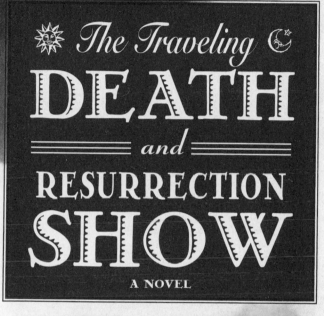

The Traveling DEATH and RESURRECTION SHOW

A NOVEL

ARIEL GORE

HarperSanFrancisco

A Division of HarperCollinsPublishers

HarperCollins books may be purchased for educational, business, or sales promotional use. For information please write: Special Markets Department, HarperCollins Publishers, 10 East 53rd Street, New York, NY 10022.

HarperCollins Web site: http://www.harpercollins.com

HarperCollins®, 📖 ®, and HarperSanFrancisco™ are trademarks of HarperCollins Publishers

FIRST EDITION

Designed by Kris Tobiassen

Library of Congress Cataloging-in-Publication Data

Gore, Ariel
The traveling Death and Resurrection Show : a novel / Ariel Gore. — 1st ed.
p. cm.
ISBN-13: 978–0–06–085428–7
ISBN-10: 0–06–085428–6
1. Catholics—Fiction. 2. Traveling theater—Fiction. 3. Belief and doubt—Fiction. 4. Christian saints—Fiction. 5. Young women—Fiction. 6. Stigmatics—Fiction. 7. Orphans—Fiction. I. Title.
PS3607.O5959T73 2006
813'.54—dc22   2005052565

06 07 08 09 10 RRD(H) 10 9 8 7 6 5 4 3 2 1

Deliver us from sour-faced saints.

— TERESA OF AVILA

My name is Frances Catherine, a.k.a. Frankka—Saint Cat onstage. With names like these, I guess it goes without saying that I'm Catholic. Or I was Catholic. *Raised* Catholic, as they say. *Lapsed* Catholic or *recovering* Catholic, like it's some kind of drug you have to quit cold turkey. Twelve steps and maybe you'll be free of the guilt that clangs like church bells. Newborn original sin washed away by a priest and I'm the only one who's mucked it up since then: *Sinner, impure, forgive me, it's all my fault.*

Was Catholic? Dream on. Fallen or faithful, what are you going to do? You're given a mythology in this life, the way you're given a body, a family, a country. You can reject it if you like—starve it, laugh in its face, run away into exile—but it's still your mythology. There's always the chance for redemption.

Things can happen so fast. One moment things are one way and the next it's all completely different—*bam*—like some kind of mystical car crash and you're so turned around you can't even pinpoint the exact moment of impact. *Was there a single moment of impact?* What about warning signs? Nothing happens without a prophecy.

I'll tell you a story.

ONE NIGHT ONLY

Whoosh. Car tires through puddles. Gasoline rainbows. Picture this: Two beat-up candy apple red hatchbacks trailing a wildflower-painted caravan down a sogged main street that creeps southward along the waterfront.

Madre Pia shouts through a cracked megaphone from the back of the caravan as we roll into town: "The lost will be saved, the saved will be amazed!" She's a vision, Madre is. Three hundred pounds of blithe drag queen cloaked in her old-school nun's habit, great bellowing penguin. "Tonight only, ladies and gentlemen! Saint Cat will manifest the wounds of Christ."

Rain-wet asphalt and dull brick buildings welcome us to empty streets. Steely June sky. We haven't seen the sun in weeks. Northwestern springtime: damp, damp.

"Come and see for yourself," Madre implores the rows of Victorian houses that cling like swallows' nests to an inland hill. "Mary Magdalen will perform her death-defying midair acrobatics. Six P.M. tonight. Astoria's own River Theater!"

A solitary freckled face peers out from a fogged pizza parlor window, kind bewildered reassurance that we haven't stumbled into a ghost town.

Madre lowers the megaphone to clear her throat, then lifts it to her berry mouth again. "Barbaro the great fire spitter all the way from Venice, Italy!"

The baby, riding with me today, whimpers in his car seat, rubs his sleepy eyes, reminds me of a clean-licked newborn kitten. Shock of black hair. Wide, dark eyes. "I'm hungry," he moans. Poor little fellow. This is our life: new day, new state, same show.

"The Virgin Mary herself will cast your fortune," Madre roars, undaunted by the city's silence. "Your destiny in Our Lady's hands!"

A towheaded little boy, maybe five years old, pale face blushed against the ocean wind, leaps from the doorway of the "I Buy Almost Anything" antique store. "Is it a circus?" he calls out, excited. But before Madre can answer him, a waif of a woman rushes out to the curb and pulls the boy back inside.

"It *is* a circus!" Madre yells to the crows perched on the roof of an old hotel. "Six P.M. tonight, the River Theater. Admission by donation. No one turned away!"

A white woman with dreadlocks stumbles out of a corner bar. "I'll be there," she promises, waving a tattooed arm before she reaches for the near cement wall to catch her balance.

"This is a show you can't miss," Madre cries with renewed enthusiasm. "One night only, ladies and gentlemen. Levitating mystics, saints performing the stigmata, Mary Magdalen flying through the air like grace itself!"

★ ★ ★

The caravan rolls to a stop in front of a little blue theater under the truss bridge. I'm driving the second hatchback, park it a few yards ahead of the others. No fans await us in handsome gray Astoria, but at least the church protesters aren't out—the sallow-eyed men and women with their dark crucifixes and homemade picket signs assuring us all eternal damnation. You'd think we were a traveling brigade of abortionists, the reception we get in some towns. *It's just a show,* I always want to tell them. *Isn't Satan up to anything real you can get your panties in a wad about?* But I stay quiet. I understand their indignation more than I'd like to admit. And sometimes, I swear I can see my grandmother's face in those crowds. I cross myself silently, then. "It's just a show," I whisper to the heavens.

A humble mural covers the side of the theater building, pictures the river itself as a stage. Spotlights hang in the clouds. A few spectators float in black inner tubes, watching a lone performer who stands atop the water like some kind of prophet. A little marquee at the corner of the painting announces our coming:

— *Tonight Only* —
THE DEATH &
RESURRECTION SHOW

I wrestle the baby from his car seat. The straps of his overalls have gotten tangled up in the belt. "C'mon, Manny. Let's go see your mama." I prop him on my hip. A few teary raindrops fall on our cheeks as we amble over to join the others.

The theater proprietor stands out on the curb to greet us, a round brunette with eyes the color of the ocean. She holds up Astoria's *Hipfish* newspaper like a prized casserole. "We made the cover," she beams.

And indeed, there we all are in full-color newsprint: Lupe and the baby stand front and center like an image of the Madonna and Child. Hefty Madre Pia in her black-and-white nun dress and model-thin platinum Magdelena, bighearted bigheads, smile like celebrities on either side. Tony, Barbaro, and Paula, shy pillars of our troupe, peer over shoulders. That's me in the back, slightly elevated, wearing a crown of thorns and too much blush, performing my signature stigmata for our high-blood-pressure publicity shot.

"They've been talking about it on the radio," the proprietor says, bouncing up and down on her toes as she talks, like maybe she's had a few too many shots of espresso. "We should get a good crowd. A pretty good crowd, anyway." *Bounce, bounce.* "This is a small town, but it'll surprise you." *Bounce, bounce.* "People really come out for our shows. You all just get in? You must be hungry." Nods all around on the hunger question, so she points us in the direction of a restaurant. "It's on us." *Bounce, bounce.* "The saints must eat."

"I'll catch up with you guys later," I say, lifting the baby from my hip and entrusting him to Lupe's waiting arms. "I'm not hungry."

Barbaro winks at me, his olive complexion so thirsty for sunlight he almost looks ill. "We will bring for you a doggie bag," he promises.

Not hungry. I imagine my fellow travelers stomping off to feast on platters of butter-drenched garlic lobster, giant bowls of broccoli with lemon sauce, thick slices of raspberry cheesecake. "Not hungry," I whisper to myself like a mantra. Truth told, I'm starving. *Willpower,* I tell myself. *Sometimes life is all about willpower.* So I grab my duffel from the trunk and head for the nearest glowing red Vacancy sign to book a few rooms for the night.

===== † =====

The wind off the river is a chill. The Lamplighter Inn only has two rooms available, so I say a quick paternoster—Our Father Who Art in Heaven—and walk on, past the Pig 'N Pancake restaurant, the smell of salty bacon winging through the damp air; past the neon-lit McDonald's arches, the squeals of children playing in a tub of colored plastic balls. The Rivershore Motel advertises cable TV and $32 doubles.

"No problem. We have space for all." The wiry Asian man behind the reservation desk smiles. "Twin bed or double? Smoking or non? You already see 1906 shipwreck?"

I answer his questions—double, non, and no—then trade him $96 cash for three keys on green plastic rings. "I like you hair," he says. "Blue streak. Very fashion." He shows me a sepia-tinted postcard picture of the old ship at Clatsop Beach to the south. "Still stay where it wreck one hundred year ago," he says. "Half cover with sand now. You go see?"

"I'd like to," I tell him, gathering up the keys and his tourist brochures.

He adjusts his glasses. "No one die there. Everybody save. You like."

* * *

Up a metal staircase and behind a pink door, the first darkened room smells of lemon disinfectant. I scan our quarters:
two square beds with polyester spreads, a small TV, a brown
minifridge, a microwave oven, a Mr. Perks coffeemaker and a
tub of dry coffee, packets of sugar and creamer, a nightstand
with a Goodwill green lamp and a copy of Gideon's Bible, a
round plastic table with a phone book and a Guest Services
binder that amounts to a few pizza parlor ads.

Towns change, but every motel room is the same.

I stretch out on the closest bed, stare up at the cottage
cheese ceiling. "Not hungry," I whisper. Mind over reality. I
close my eyes. *Not hungry.* But just as I manage to push the
food fantasies out of my consciousness, a new doubt starts
pecking at the corner of my mind. Maybe all these years on
the road are finally starting to take their toll. We've criss-
crossed the country two dozen times. Everyone but
Magdelena and Madre has stopped reading the previews and
the write-ups. As we roll into each new town, Madre Pia's
great bellowing promise, "The lost will be saved, the saved
will be amazed!" But I don't know anymore which group I
belong to. Lost or saved? Twenty-eight years old, and out of
the quick blue nowhere it occurs to me: With each passing
performance, I feel less sure of who I am.

Chapter 2
DESTINY

Sometimes when I walk through the rain, I know that each drop that falls on me wasn't meant to fall on anybody else. Other times I take an umbrella to shield myself from the randomness.

You are the product of your upbringing. You are the product of your society. You are the product of your times. You are the product of your astrological chart. You are the product of peer pressure. You are the product of your maker. *Which is it?* Maybe God was really hungover the morning he stumbled out of bed and created me.

I peel myself off the motel mattress, fish around in my duffel for my saint book and pen, sit down at the white plastic table to scrawl myself a story.

Julian the Poor
(IF YOU NEED SHELTER)

A.K.A. Julian the Hospitaller
FEAST DAY: February 12
SYMBOLS: a hawk, a stag, an oar

Now imagine Saint Julian the Poor as a kid—before sainthood, before poverty. Thirteenth-century mama's boy dressed in velvet and silk. An only child, he dined with all the fat cats of Normandy and Angiers at tables draped with linen damask. Even adolescence didn't make young Julian's feet itch with rebellion, but life had more in store for him than crab cakes and cranberry cocktails.

The day started like any other: A casual morning. Catered lunch with the king. Champagne and a light dessert. A few of the guys were headed out to hunt. *Would Julian like to join them?*

"Of course!" Julian loved nothing more than a hunt.

"Cheers and see you later, then." *Ting, ting.*

But those forests of western France can be dense, the trails narrow. Maybe Julian stopped to admire a beetle. Maybe he fell into an indistinct daydream. It seemed only a moment, but suddenly everything was deathly quiet. Just the slow steady breathing of his own horse. A far stream. "Hey, guys?" he called out.

No answer.

A fork in the path. Right or left? The rustle of a lizard darting through the bramble. A rock sparrow's call. "Hey, guys?"

Left. Maybe left. He galloped, hoping to catch up with his friends, but only found himself in an unfamiliar clearing.

"Hello?"

That's when he saw it, just ahead of him between the broad-leaves: a resting woodland deer.

It almost seemed too easy, but Julian dismounted and grabbed his bow. As he drew back, his mind danced. He'd find his way home, carrying the beast on his horse. He'd tell a fantastic tale about how he'd intentionally split off from the group, how he'd artfully tracked the animal.

Release. *Yes!* Right in the neck. But the deer didn't die instantly. Instead, it turned to face Julian. And that animal had the eyes of a human.

"What do you want with me?" the deer asked, its voice thick with disdain. "Was I troubling you so much, resting here?"

Julian stared, speechless.

The deer glared at him. "You've killed me, but now I'll tell you *your* fate. You'll kill your mother and father, too—with a single blow." With that, the animal closed its eyes.

The only sound Julian could hear was the quickening of his own heartbeat. *I could never kill my parents.* Maybe in that long moment, Julian could have sworn off violence of every kind, but he was only a boy. All he could think was: *Run away. Disappear.*

"Julian! Julian!"

He stood statue still.

The voices came closer. "Julian! Julian!" Then farther away. "Julian! Julian!"

He crept through the darkening wood until even the memory of those voices seemed to fade, but the deer's gaze stayed with him—those wide and piercing brown eyes. He walked on.

In the first village he came to, Julian sold his horse and clothes. When the money ran out, he wandered in rags, begging sustenance. Finally he made his way to Rome to seek counsel from the pope, but the pope just so happened to be recruiting for the Crusades that summer. Off Julian went in uniform: violence, violence.

He distinguished himself in battle, murdering for a cause he could imagine worth murdering for. Grandmothers wept. Julian was knighted, then made a count. He married a young widow named Clarisse, and the couple lived in carefree oblivion for two gorgeous years. But who ever cheated fate by running away?

"Julian? Julian!"

His parents had never given up, and now at last they had a solid lead: the brave count called Julian. Mother and father disguised themselves as pilgrims, traveled to their son's castle.

Clarisse welcomed them, generous-hearted woman. "Come in," she said. "You must be tired. Here. Rest in our bed. Julian will be back from his hunt by evening."

When Julian got home, he thought it strange that Clarisse wasn't at the door to meet him. First stir of apprehension. Maybe she'd decided to take a nap? But when he opened the door to their room and saw two bodies in their bed, his confusion mutated into rage. Julian drew his sword before asking questions, and he killed his parents with a single blow.

Only when he realized what he'd done did it all hit him: the horror of violence. A lifetime of regret welled up like bile.

Grief-stricken and lost, Julian again traded his finery for rags and went into exile, this time with his wife—and not so much to run away but to do penance. The two traveled from village to village, eventually settling in the worst part of the worst town, where thieves and thugs ruled the streets and the river raged treacherous. They built a humble shelter, dedicated their lives to ferrying drifters on their way. They harbored runaways, refugees, and traveling performers, spent their days in service and their nights around the fire, listening to Irish fiddles and Gypsy guitar.

One dark midnight, a voice from the other side of the river woke them. "I need a lift!"

Julian dragged himself out of bed, paddled across.

An exhausted leper climbed aboard. "I need shelter, too," he whispered.

Clarisse prepared a light dinner for the traveler. Bread and tomatoes. "Can we help you with anything else?"

"Well, yes," the man said. "I'd like to sleep with you, Clarisse."

Julian's face reddened. *The nerve!*

But Clarisse just smiled. "Let me show you the bed."

Julian clenched his teeth. *Penance,* he whispered to himself. *Sometimes life is all about penance.*

Clarisse said good-night to her husband and went to join the tired stranger, but she found the bed empty.

From outside, they heard the traveler's voice: "You have been tested. Your sins are forgiven." Then the angel vanished, leaving the couple so bewildered they hardly knew where they were.

Forgiven, Julian and Clarisse carried on with their lives of service, ferrying travelers across the river and harboring the road-weary.

Late one night, moonlight bathing their tiny room in a silvery iridescence, thieves broke in and killed them both with a single blow. But travel to that river crossing even today and you'll find nothing but miracles. Anywhere you are in the world, if you need shelter, just think of Julian and Clarisse. Say a quick paternoster, and you'll find what you need.

Patron saint of innkeepers and traveling performers, Julian will serve you well. Say thanks by giving away something you can't imagine living without. Trade all your weapons of violence and privilege for musical instruments, and welcome the winds of change into your small world.

Back at the River Theater an hour before showtime, I unfurl the indigo backdrop, help Barbaro move platforms.

Paula rigs ropes and swings. "It's brilliant to be in a real theater," she sighs.

The place isn't huge, seats maybe a hundred, but it smells of old upholstery and fresh paint. *A real theater.* Most nights, Paula hangs the trapeze from café ceiling beams or hauls out the freestanding rig. We perform over the hiss and roar of espresso machines and the clink of beer glasses. Tonight Tony sits at the edge of the stage, testing his amps, serious-excited. Lupe braids her hair into a long rope. Madre Pia calls out directions from the back of the house: "That platform needs to be angled to the right. I'd turn your volume up, Tony. Lupe? You'll set your booth up in the lobby?"

Even the baby feels important. He dances and spins onstage, belting out the *Sesame Street* theme song. *The baby.* I guess he's not so little anymore. It hardly seems more than a few rainy months since he joined us—a double-chinned infant

attached only to his mother's tit, oblivious to both the newness
and boredom of the road. Time boggles the mind. Little tub-
ster, he turned four in March, knows the show by heart. He
stands boldly against this knotted world we all pray against
prayer will somehow rise to meet his enthusiasm for it. "To get
to Sesame Street!" He applauds for himself, takes a bow.

Backstage, I trade my jeans and T-shirt for a loose white
dress, futz with my hair. Should I wear it up or down? It actually looks better up, but I think I look younger with it down,
so I leave it brushing my shoulders. *How many years did I spend
waiting for my life to start, only to be reduced to longing for those
waiting years at the first sign of age?*

Magdelena spreads a thick layer of foundation over her
porcelain skin, paints her plum lips, pulls her blond hair into a
tight ponytail. Her lit cigarette balances on the edge of a black
makeup table. "Too bad we're only here one night," she says,
then knocks back a shot of brandy, picks up her cigarette, and
flicks the ash into her empty glass. "We could do a real run in
a theater like this."

I reach to borrow her Great Lash.

A real run. If only we could froth up the crowds for it.
A town of ten thousand—even a generous town of ten
thousand—can't be expected to sit through more than a
night or two of miracles.

"You ever get the feeling that your destiny is way bigger
than the life you're living?" Magdelena asks. She's been coming up with Big Questions ever since she turned thirty. "I
used to think that destiny just happened—like you couldn't
control it one way or the other—but what if it's possible to
just completely miss your boat?" She applies her kohl eyeliner

with the precision of a calligrapher. "I mean, what if your ship came in on the very morning you slept in and didn't make it out to the dock? Or what if you thought something was your ship and you got on, but it totally wasn't your ship? What if you were just spacing out and you missed your destiny?"

I wonder if Magdelena's thinking about the man she left when we took our show on the road, the one who soon married her look-alike and settled down to children and office work. Or maybe it's dawning on her that she might never get famous. "You only get one chance at this life," she says gravely, then winks at me. "No room to screw up."

I think to tell Magdelena about my own creeping anxiety and road weariness, but just then Madre Pia peers around the black door frame. "You ladies ready?" And for the first time all season, a shimmer of stage fright flashes across my chest. I look down at my palms. How strange that these tiny pink scars have become my way in this world.

Chapter 3
HUNGER

What can I tell you about my particular talent? Doesn't every child deform herself somehow in order to get what she needs from the strange grown-ups who tower over her, offering and withholding love and sustenance at chaotic intervals? Doesn't everyone learn, eventually, to trace patterns from that chaos?

You're no saint yourself. Surely you, too, developed some ploy—maybe a series of ploys—to melt your father's icy gaze, your mother's waxy distraction. Maybe you learned a little dance that grabbed her attention just as she got that first twinkle of a faraway look in her eye, nostalgia for a season before you were born. Olives heavy on the branch.

As you grew, taller every year but still helpless and dependent, you learned the perfect joke that could turn base rage into laughter. You made your own kind of sense of the grown-ups' world, learned to tease affection from annoyance, draw milk from exhaustion. It's survival, nothing to be ashamed of.

My trick to stave off the grown-ups' depression was unusually graphic, I'll give you that. Or—who knows?—maybe it isn't unusual at all. Maybe it's as common as sin. Maybe it's just one of those things that goes unconfessed. In any case, I've never actually met anyone else who'll admit to the ability to bleed at will.

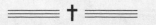

I've tried a hundred times to pinpoint the exact memory-scene—the first time I performed my trick. But my recollections refuse to stack themselves into neat chronological piles. My childhood is a shuffle of undated events and images. No matter. I'll pull a card. We'll say I'm seven years old. We'll call it the first time:

I stood barefoot in our narrow green-carpeted living room.
   God, I'm hungry.
   My grandmother wept in her tattered gold armchair, the light from the small TV screen flickering like a candle.
   I fixed my gaze on the wall behind her, on the rosaries that hung from rusted nails, then on the bright Easter portrait of Our Lord above. His blessed face shone like the sun behind him, and I knew—I could just tell—Our Good Lord was well fed. He stood with his hands outstretched, palms still bleeding from his Good Friday ordeal.
   My stomach growled. I stared helplessly at the image of Our Lord, wished he'd show up, just this once, to multiply a

few fish and loaves like he did in the olden days, but I knew it was useless. Even multiplication couldn't help me now. Zero times zero equals zero. Empty refrigerator.

I could've gotten something myself, I knew I could, but I also knew I wasn't allowed to cross the street to Kim's Groceries by myself, wasn't allowed to climb up onto the countertop in our closet of a kitchen to reach the raw potatoes in the high cupboard.

I was a patient girl, but my grandmother had been crouched like this for days, crying "What kind of God?" and "What kind of God?"

I closed my eyes, stretched my arms out like the image of our resurrected Lord. I forced all the pain and strength of my hunger up from my belly, up into my head, then out, out, out through my limbs. I concentrated on my hands. The dull ache of my hunger felt like nails.

"Nana," I whispered, half-opening my eyes.

As she lifted her head, I pressed my starvation out through the centers of my palms. I trembled, just a little, as my hunger oozed like blood, perfect red teardrops from my wounds. I held the pose for a long minute, then fell to my knees—half from exhaustion, half for dramatic effect.

"My child!" My grandmother rushed to my side. "My child." She smelled of rose water and sour sweat. "Dear God, forgive me my doubt."

A rustling and a clanging from the kitchen. The sound of my own breath as I lay curled on the avocado carpet. The half-cooked potato slices revived me easily, and by evening the cupboards and fridge filled with dried pasta, fresh tomatoes, green olives, gorgonzola cheese, canned peaches.

That night, Nana and I walked arm in arm under the magnolias through the warm autumn darkness to midnight mass, full of love and compassion for Our Lord and God.

As my grandmother knelt in the pew, whispering Hail Mary and mea culpa, I silently made my peace with the lit-glass image of Our Savior on the far-facing wall. "Jesus," I whispered, "I sure hope you don't mind me doing the blood trick, but when Nana needs a sign and you're too busy to give her one, I figure you won't be angry if I play at being risen. If it makes you angry, Lord, then maybe you can give me a sign—thunder or lightning or something—and I swear I'll stop doing it right then. But how about let's say, just between you and me, if you're silent, that means it's okay? Maybe you're even a little bit pleased that I've figured out how to bring Nana back to you when she starts to get so sad? I mean, it's real hard for her down here, Lord. She does believe in you, honest. She's as faithful as they come. She just needs signs these days. You can understand that, can't you? It's been a terrible test for her, you taking back my mom and dad. I know you're real busy, Lord, but . . ."

Our Savior hung silent in his stained glass pane and I knew I should confess my trick to Father Michaels, but somehow I knew, too, that I couldn't, that no good ever came of a child kneeling in a dark confessional and telling the truth. How could I expect Father Michaels to understand that my trick was neither blaspheme nor miracle? I was hungry, that's all. And a hungry child can make herself bleed, make herself do a lot of things.

Chapter 4

WE WELCOME YOU
TO THE REALM
OF THE BLESSED

All lights out.

Close your eyes.

Madre Pia's great booming voice explodes into the black: "In the beginning God created the heavens and the earth. And the earth was without form, and void. And darkness was upon the face of the deep. And the spirit moved across the face of the waters. And God said, *Let there be light!*"

A billow of flame bursts from a dark figure stage left.

Madre lifts her large hands and the lights rise, illuminating the strange beauty Saint Paula the Bearded as she begins to sing her low sweet hymn.

Tony's hypnotic bass line starts so low and builds so slow, his intro is almost over before you realize it's more than auditory hallucination. He picks up his tenor sax, moves effortlessly into "A Love Supreme."

Madre continues in a raspy whisper, telling how God separated the light from the darkness, the firmament from the earth, the waters from the waters; how God created all the living things, plants yielding seeds and trees bearing luscious fruits, birds flying upward to the heavens, great sea monsters and fish, creeping things and cattle. "But, alas," Madre hums as Tony wraps the intro of his jazz suite, "even with all of these living things, God felt lonely. The green plants thrived in the moist earth, the birds danced across the sky, and the stars sang in the firmament; the creatures of the water swam in great schools, and the creeping things prowled across fertile and arid lands, contented. But for all these grand theatrics, where was the audience? God prayed for company, for spectators and fellow storytellers, and there was evening and morning and lo! God had an idea. *Let us make human beings, in our image, after our likeness.* So God created us, male and female God created us, and God blessed us and said: *Be fruitful and multiply.*"

Barbaro the stranger is the shadowed figure tiptoeing across the stage, a canvas bag slung over his shoulder. Tall and muscular, he has the light step of a dancer, the strong jaw of someone who could teach you how to laugh. He glances right and left, nervous and searching.

"We welcome you to the realm of the blessed," Madre whispers unseen.

Barbaro the stranger gazes upward, confused, as if he's looking for a body to go with the voice. He takes cover in a far corner of the stage.

No words necessary now, the saxophone rises.

Magdelena, wrapped in a tight orange bodysuit, leaps from the highest platform, grabs her trapeze bar, swings up into a double somersault. She loves to fly, Magdelena does. She soars across the stage like a bird in the firmament. Unprotected by safety lunges, she lives for the crowd's awe-drenched gasp, hangs in the suspended pleasure of her aerial ballet.

Barbaro the stranger watches, reverent. He reaches up as if longing to join her in the sky, but Lupe, dazzling in her sequined virgin blue dress against the darker blue backdrop, shoos the stranger away. She waits to catch Magdelena's slim body as—*swoop*—she somersaults back to earth.

The curtain falls.

In the dressing room, I hand Manny off to Paula, leave them singing the ABCs as I join Magdelena, Tony, and Lupe onstage. The curtain rises on our small circle of friends singing off-key and clowning, making music and dancing, drinking and laughing.

Barbaro the stranger stands in the shadows, watching, but each time he starts to approach, we push him away. Outsider. He rustles in his bag, produces a carnival mask, tries to get the revelers' attention, but we're focused on our own small world.

Tony picks up his saxophone, plays us a few notes, then launches into a narcotic lullaby.

The friends sway sleepy, lights dim.

All quiet in the theater. *Shhh.*

Then a sudden clamor from stage right. Madre's heavy footfalls. She's all in black as she grabs me from my sleep and drags me away. Barbaro the stranger is the only witness. He rushes to rouse the others from their heavy sleep. He points, panicked.

The curtain falls.

I take my place now, center stage.

Curtain up and the lights are a blinding wall of white. I extend my arms, crosslike.

The bass line like a heartbeat and the friends come rushing with the stranger, but they're too late.

I close my eyes and force my appetite up from my belly and into my head, my mind empty of everything but the hunger. I press it out through my shoulders, through my muscles and veins. I feel the blood as it courses down my arms like a lava flow. I tremble, just a little, before my palms split open.

A gasp from the back of the house.

A sudden flash, unexpected, and I'm distracted, but just for a moment. I hold my pose as Tony's molten sax climbs, then collapse into Lupe's arms.

A moan from the front row. Lights lowered and blue.

A great wind-sound and here's Barbaro the stranger, dancing a slow dance around my body and blowing flames of grief, illuminating the dusky stage like a thousand halos.

Saint Paula sings, this time like a mantra with the sax to guide her.

My companions watch as the stranger pours wine red juice into my mouth. Madre Pia, dressed in white now, lifts me from behind and I stand, resurrected. Madre keeps rising: up, up, up. She hovers above the stage, shining like a prophet in her levitation. "Blessed are the poor in spirit," she whispers, "for theirs is the kingdom of heaven. Blessed are they who mourn, for they shall be comforted. Blessed are those who hunger and thirst for righteousness, for they shall be filled . . . Blessed are the peacemakers, and the tree-sitters, and the cross-dressers, and the beggars, and the loafers, and the gamblers, and the musicians, and the circus performers, and the mothers, and the children, and the teachers, and the artists, and the workers, and the seekers, and the wanderers—for we shall all be called the children of God." Madre rises higher. "Embrace the mystery!"

Now Barbaro is one of us, blowing his wild flames as Magdelena flies, full faith in her catcher.

All of us onstage, the baby watches from behind the curtain, and Paula croons her final winged traveling song, breaking the trance.

Shooting stars of applause and "Hallelujah!"

The audience doesn't want to leave. They only file out when all the house lights come up and fortunes are promised in the lobby.

===== † =====

We all know the drill by now.

My fellow travelers break down the set.

Lupe sits at her card table, studying palms and handing out predictions of romance and abundance.

No one expects me to work after a performance. "Let her eat," they say.

I devour the cold fish-and-chips from Barbaro's greasy doggie bag, douse every bite with malt vinegar from little plastic packets, lick the salt from my fingers, dig into the plastic container of mustard greens.

"Taste good?" Manny wants to know. He's a dimple-cheeked cherub.

"Divine," I mumble, stuffing a few more fries into my mouth.

"You talk with your mouth full!" he squeals, delighted. He climbs up onto a wooden chair. "Butt-ass!" he screams, leaping off the chair. He lands on the floor with a thud. "I'm a superhero," he insists, scrambling to his feet. He climbs back up onto the chair, looks suddenly serious. "In the beginning, God created the heavens and the earth," he says in a low voice, mocking Madre Pia. "The earth was without form and void!" He jumps off the chair again, this time flailing a little before he hits the floor. He stumbles, falls forward, starts to cry. "Where's my mommy?" he sobs.

I shove the last fries into my mouth. "She's out in the lobby, honey. Are you okay?" I move to comfort him, but he takes off wailing, "Moooommmy!"

Sometimes we all feel like Manny's parents. We feed him jelly sandwiches and applesauce from glass jars, read him cardboard books about animals that can talk, help him piece LEGOs into spaceships. We carry him on our shoulders and hips, but we're fooling ourselves. When it comes to a skinned knee or a bumped head, there's only one woman in his life: "Moooommmy!" Who else but Lupe could rock him just so, coo as if no one else had ever suffered?

I lick the salt and grease from the bag. *Delicious.*

★　★　★

"Want to get a drink across the street, hmm?" Madre Pia asks. She hasn't washed off her makeup, but she's wearing a simple white T-shirt and big black overalls. Her shoulder-length brown hair is damaged from too much dyeing and straightening. "Magdelena and Paula are coming."

I shrug. "Did we make any money?"

"Five hundred bucks." Madre smacks her lips.

Not bad. Fifty for each of us and the rest for the travel fund. "Then why not?"

A ruddy-faced drunk dances in the doorway of the Worker's Bar. "We're pregnant!" he sings. "I'm fifty years old and I'm finally going to be a dad!"

We laugh, congratulate him as we push past.

The place is smoky but well lit. A few dozen locals in jeans and flannel shirts sip their pints and gossip.

We sit down at the bar, order three Vodka crans and a double shot of whiskey for Paula. "Best show we've done in years," Magdelena sighs. And she's right. On an average night we're musicians and magicians, entertaining the worn-out hippies, lapsed Catholics, and world-weary punks of small-town America. Everything is plagiarized, but creative plagiarism can be amusing. On a good night, we perform our acts more seamlessly. There's nothing like a resurrection metaphor—a revelation of transcendent spirit—to soften granite hearts. But on a night like tonight, something exquisite rises from our shoulders. We're not performing anymore. We ascend like water walkers, and the spectators need no inner tubes. If Magdelena can fly without wings, if Madre can levitate three hundred pounds, if Barbaro can breathe an inferno, if Paula can grow a beard and still sing like Norah

Jones, if Tony can recall the masterpiece of "A Love Supreme," if I can bleed without dying, rise up like some kind of phoenix, then surely even you can transcend your cobalt depression, get sober, shrink a tumor, remember the way you once loved life, burn out your tangled nest of regrets.

"Gentleman on the other side of the bar just bought y'all another round," the bartender tells us, pointing to the father-to-be from outside.

"Those are the weird girls who laughed at me," he says.

We weren't laughing *at* him, exactly, but who's going to argue with free drinks?

"I'll laugh at you if you'll buy me a drink," someone calls out, and maybe Dad just got paid because he doesn't hesitate. "All right, another drink!"

An old man with a long white beard studies us from the other end of the bar. "Girls?" he wrinkles his bulbous nose. "Where y'all from?" his voice is all gravel.

"San Francisco," Madre offers for simplicity's sake.

The old man nods into his beer like he figured as much, lights a GPC cigarette. "Time was they called Astoria San Francisco of Oregon," he says, then shakes his head. "San *Fran*-cisco. I guess down there you gotta turn 'em upside down to figure if they're a boy or a girl."

Paula fidgets with her studded belt, nervous, but Madre just laughs. "And up here I guess you don't quit smoking 'til you're dead."

The old man chuckles, won over just like that.

And now the bartender's passing out boards for meat bingo.

"Meat bingo?" Magdelena raises an eyebrow.

"Yeah. It's just like bingo, but we play for meat." He holds up a plastic- and Styrofoam-wrapped raw steak.

I'm still hungry, actually thinking about how that steak might taste cooked in the motel microwave, when the theater proprietor rushes in, waving a ripped piece of yellow paper. "I'm so glad I caught you! Someone called after the show." *Bounce. Bounce.* "A reporter from the *L.A. Times* wants to meet you at the Pig 'N Pancake for breakfast!"

"The *L.A. Times?*" Magdelena's bright blue eyes widen.

"Huge circulation," Madre beams.

Quiet Paula smiles, too. "The *L.A. Times?*"

"I'm really glad I caught you," the proprietor says again. *Bounce.*

Another round of drinks, then.

Magdelena pulls the hair band from her ponytail, lets her blond hair fall on her shoulders, floats from her barstool, and lifts her arms over her head. "I'm a street light," she sings. "I want to be a star! I want to inspire and show off and get a makeover and grace the covers of magazines like Drew Barrymore."

"It's just a reporter," I mumble.

"Oh, don't be a pill, Frankka."

I hadn't noticed the jukebox before, but now Dolly Parton's singing about a hard candy Christmas and I guess Magdelena's right. *Don't be a pill.* I'm getting buzzed. Maybe my afternoon worries were nothing more than hunger. If news of a reporter from the *L.A. Times* can make my fellow travelers this happy, maybe it doesn't matter if we're lost or saved.

"B-6!" the bingo caller cries.

Raw steak for the dad-to-be.

We down our drinks like Kool Aid, trip home to the Rivershore Motel to share the good news.

Chapter 5

THE REPORTER SHOWS UP

The reporter shows up in high-heeled boots, a long denim skirt, a black V-neck sweater. The clip-clop of her steps as she approaches our green vinyl booth says "downtown," says "professional," says "I'm a long way from L.A. and this better be good." The Versace sunglasses perched on her head must be there to keep the sandy blond hair out of her eyes because there isn't any danger of the sun showing its face today.

Madre stands, offers Miss L.A. the empty chair. "Long drive?"

Magdelena looks a little crestfallen when the reporter admits she didn't come all this way just for us.

"I was down in southern Oregon," she says. "My editor thought the two wildfires would merge. All the meteorology reports pointed to disaster. I'm Lifestyle, so I was there to hit the human interest angle—families who've lost everything,

missing dogs, college kids last seen in the fire zone. But . . ."
She shrugs. "Fire's ninety-five percent contained. So I kept
driving. I actually caught your show last night. I ran the idea
past my editor. You're performing in L.A. this weekend, right?
We can promo it."

"That's awesome," Magdelena coos, easily placated.

"We are honored by your visit," Barbaro chimes in. "I
hope you will find our brigade as wondrous as any forest fire."

Little plush and porcelain pig knickknacks clutter shelves
all over the restaurant.

"Anyway," the reporter says, opening her notebook, "I'm
Judy." She taps her long, French-manicured nails on the table.
"I was hoping you could just give me some background.
How the show got started. How you all met. Then I'd like to
interview each of you individually if that's all right."

Nods all around.

I sip my black coffee.

Tony's the first one to pipe up, offering Judy the press
release version of our history. It's not too far from the truth, his
story, but most of us have a little something to hide. There's
Barbaro and his nonexistent green card, Lupe on the run from
her husband. Magdelena doesn't want anyone to know she's
over thirty. And then there's me—the secret of my trick.

═══ † ═══

Tony and I were sitting on the big Mexican rug in the living
room of our old student house, a grand Victorian rental that
creaked and leaked through the winter. This was years ago,
and about a month after I'd dropped out of college. He

offered me a joint. I hardly ever smoked, but I accepted with a shrug. *Why not?* The inhale tasted like torment. I remembered why I avoided the stuff—reminded me of all the philosophy students with their heads in the clouds, tripping on "God is Dead" and the dehumanization of humanity and the sad truth that no matter how much you smoked, things weren't okay.

I'd turned to Socrates, Nietzsche, and Confucius because I could accept neither the nihilism of science nor the dogma of religion, but the philosophy department turned out to be just another tangled mess of words.

"Language is meaningless!" my favorite professor cried out in lecture hall the morning before he shot himself in the head. "There is no shared context." Tears rolled down his sunwrinkled face.

Imagine dying for lack of a shared context. Almost as absurd as committing murder for lack of a shared vision of God. Still, I wished I'd understood how desperate he felt that morning. Instead, I wrote his words in my red spiral notebook. *Language is meaningless. There is no shared context.* As if we were going to be quizzed on that.

I tried to focus on Tony now, his coffee black skin, angular features, the stubble on his chin, hair cut so short you couldn't tell it was curly, the words he strung together into a rambling monologue. The two of us had dated briefly when Tony first moved in to the student house, but our kisses always felt awkward. The sex was sweet but passionless. When he finally said, "I'm attracted to you, Frankka, but I don't think it's romantic," I had to agree. Now he spoke of lucid dreams and low-impact living. He'd recently quit his job, didn't want to look for another. He'd taken a vow not to cause suffering. Seems simple enough: *So That I May Not Cause Suffering.* And at first it had been something like simple. His goal was to contain his habitual mean streak, the little comments that passed for humor but were intended to belittle: *Nice shirt. Ha, ha. You can't really like that band. Ha, ha. You're not that fat. Ha, ha. I guess you haven't read Ginsburg.* Simple, but pretty soon just containing his mean streak hardly seemed enough. He learned to hold his tongue when he wanted to use words to wound, but as soon as he'd gotten a handle on that, other ways in which he caused suffering presented themselves. He had to stop eating meat, of course. Couldn't even kill a spider. He had to close his bank accounts. His savings were being invested in unjust enterprises all over the world. He stopped buying clothes made in sweatshops. He'd never realized how hard it was to find a T-shirt that hadn't been dyed or sewn in Thailand or Honduras. He couldn't keep his job at the flower stand—workers in Ecuador were being poisoned to harvest those gorgeous, scentless roses. He had to convert his little diesel hatchback to run on grease because he saw the blood of innocents flowing from every gas pump. *So That I May Not Cause Suffering.* Within a month, Tony had become just another organic-cotton-wearing unemployed vegetarian street musician who couldn't pay the rent on his six-foot-by-six-foot walk-in closet-turned-bedroom three blocks from the beach in Santa Cruz, California.

So here's Tony. He doesn't ask anything of this world beyond sustenance. All he wants is to honor this vow: *So That I May Not Cause Suffering.*

Fairly traded coffee: $10.99/lb.
Closet of a room in the student house: $515/mo.
Sweatshop-free organic cotton apparel: $41/outfit
Share of utilities even though he uses almost no electricity:
   $34/mo.
Food bill at the co-op: $65/mo.
Available jobs for a man without a college degree who refuses
   to cause suffering: 0

He said, "If you don't want to work for The Man, you have to have some kind of a talent, you know? I play my saxophone on the street corner and people like it all right, but it's not like I can play the guitar and sing. Sax and bass are really kind of useless if you have to make a living busking."

I gazed up at the water-damaged ceiling, ravenous. I couldn't remember the last time I'd been this hungry. And all at once my appetite seemed funny. Hilarious, in fact. "I have a talent!" I blurted out.

"What is it?"

I wasn't sure if I could do it in front of Tony. I'd never performed my trick for anyone but my grandmother—denied it, in fact. When Nana took me to Father Michaels to convince him of the miracle, I'd stood there in front of his big oak desk with my arms outstretched, poker-faced, willing nothing to happen.

"Batty old woman," I heard him mutter as we left the office.

I walked out of the church building, head down, sure my grandmother would be angry with me for making her look like such an idiot in front of the new priest, but she just squeezed my hand. "Our Lord works in mysterious ways, my child."

I took a deep breath, stood up, and faced Tony. I closed my eyes, concentrated on the sheer emptiness of my belly. I forced the dull ache up, up, up, then out. *Could I even still do it?* I concentrated on my palms, hot in the center.

Tony stared, slack-jawed. "Holy shit, Frankka."

I fell to my knees.

Tony rushed to my side. "Oh, my God, are you okay?" He lifted my hand, pressed his thumb into my palm. "That's so bizarre."

"You have to feed me something," I managed.

Awestruck, Tony scrambled into the kitchen. As he fed me organic banana chips from their crinkly plastic bag, he wanted to know everything. "What *is* it?"

"It's just a trick," I said, sitting up. "Like some people can move their eyeballs independently of one another."

"No," he whispered. "Are you, like, a saint or something?"

"Yeah," I laughed. "Hadn't you noticed?" It had been Tony, not forty-eight hours earlier, who'd called me the worst cynic he'd ever met. I said, "Anyway, Jesus wasn't actually crucified through his palms. The way they used to crucify people—they used square nails and pounded them through the wrists and ankles. His palms only bleed in the pictures. Real saints get the stigmata because they identify so totally with Christ's suffering. I just learned to do it for attention."

Tony shook his head. "I'm serious, Frankka. People would pay clean money to see that."

Something like panic shot through me, like maybe I shouldn't have let Tony in on my talent. "No way. It's a secret." I clenched my fists. "Church people freak out over this shit."

But Tony just smiled. "It's not like anyone's gonna believe it's real. They'll just think it's a wild magic trick."

"Then why would they want to see it?"

"Because it's an awesome magic trick, Frankka. One of the best I've seen. It could be some kind of miracle performance, you know? Or, I don't know, part of a cabaret."

"What would we call it?" I laughed. "*The Death & Resurrection Show?*"

So, I'd given Tony the demonstration of my talent and the whim to call it *The Death & Resurrection Show,* but he's the one who ran with the idea. By morning, the little seed I'd planted in him had grown into a blossoming scarlet-flowered tree. "We can't just go around having you bleed," he said, stirring organic honey into his chai tea. "It has to be a real show. Like we've got to have a few performers, and we've got to have some kind of a story line. The obvious thing to do would be to go completely biblical, but I'm thinking deeper than that, you know? I'm thinking biblical, I'm thinking kabbalistic, I'm thinking alchemical, I'm thinking classical Greek. I'm thinking Eleusinian mysteries, you know? I'm thinking Isis, Dionysus, Demeter, Persephone, Jesus—all of them. Everyone who ever really *understood* rebirth. Or maybe burlesque. Greek burlesque. Do you know what I'm talking about, Frankka?"

I did and I didn't. I'd never been that into Greek mythology, but it made me happy to see Tony so fired up. I wasn't sure if I'd be able to perform my trick publicly, either, but I agreed to give it a try. *What else is a dropout from the philosophy department with a knack for bleeding going to do?*

And by nightfall, the idea had started to grow on me. There was something absurd and alluring about it—we'd sell everything we had for next to nothing at a huge yard sale, give up the comfort of our own Rock Soft futons, ignore all

the voices that say You Can't Do That, and trust that the world
would somehow support us.

Right away, Tony thought of his friend Magdelena, trapeze
artist and all-around diva. They'd met at the Berklee College
of Music in Boston, had been an item for a few months, were
both in California now, unemployed. Tony said, "You've got
star talent, Frankka, but every road show needs at least one
member with an ego that stretches to the heavens."

Magdelena showed up on a Thursday, wearing fishnet
stockings and a peacock feather in her hair, looked me up and
down just to make sure she was the more beautiful. The three of
us rehearsed in that living room for hours and days, our other
roommates and their lovers drifting in and out like stray cats.

The problem, it turned out, wasn't that I had any difficulty performing in front of friends or strangers, but that I
had to be legitimately hungry to get the blood moving. After
a meal—even after a snack—no blood would flow. We exper-
imented with degrees of starvation. If I ate a light breakfast
just before 9:00 in the morning, I could achieve the stigmata
by about 6:00 P.M. No breakfast at all, and I'd be good to go
by 4:00 in the afternoon. If we were going to take this show
on the road, careful attention would have to be paid to my
diet and nutrition.

Mercifully, Magdelena had been anorexic for most of her
teen years and knew the precise caloric margin between livable hunger and the kind of famine that can land a girl in the
hospital. "It's all in the nutrient-rich vegetables," she assured

me, and within a few days she'd concocted a sweet beet-apple juice that looked like communion wine and revived me easily. After rehearsals, she fed me plates of lentils and mustard greens.

By February, we weren't quite ready to go, but rent was due and we had no money, so we sold everything and packed up the rest, hung a St. Christopher medal from the rearview mirror of Tony's little red grease-mobile, and headed off to perform on sidewalks and in a few cafés from Santa Cruz to San Diego, wowing the street kids and horrifying well-heeled tourists along the way.

At a pizza parlor in Mesa, Arizona, we found Madre Pia—just Pia at the time—a washed-up transvestite with big dreams. She'd planned to save her counter tips and move to San Francisco to launch a comedy levitation drag show. It wasn't a chance meeting. A hippie chick in Orange County had seen our little show. "You have to meet my friend Pia," she insisted. Then her beeper went off. "Oh, my God, it's synchronicity! I bet that's Pia now!" But it was the girl's mother. "Anyway. Pia. She's huge, but she can actually levitate. Swear to God. She used to perform in this Latin drag show in Santa Fe, but she isn't Latin and plus some serious I-don't-know-what shit went down between the performers, and anyway, the thing completely fell apart and she just got superdepressed. She hasn't been performing for—I don't know—a year? Anyway. She's doing nothing. Living nowhere. God, you'd love her."

The hippie girl's pitch didn't seem all that promising, but on our way out of Phoenix, Tony called and booked a last-minute performance at L.J.'s Pizza.

Now, serving pizza isn't nothing, and Mesa isn't nowhere, but for someone like Pia it might as well have been.

"We're going east, not west," Tony explained over iceberg lettuce drowned in blue cheese dressing after our little show. "But if you can really levitate, we'd sure consider having you along."

Pia didn't say yes or no, just, "I know where we can get a really cool painted caravan."

The difference between Pia and the rest of us, it turned out, was that Pia was a full-fledged, card-carrying believer. Her card was red and white and wallet sized. She'd ordered it from the back cover of the *National Inquirer*. A real live Certificate of Ordination from the Order of the Holy Spirit.

Tony's eyes brightened as he turned the card over in his hand. "This is a joke, right?"

It was and it wasn't.

"How can you believe in the Bible when it's so homophobic?" Tony wanted to know.

Pia shrugged. "I wondered about that, too, so I asked God."

"And?"

"God said, 'Hey, the Bible's got plenty of good words in it, Pia, but an oak tree praises me by being an oak tree. An oak tree doesn't try to be a pine, now, does it?' "

"How'd you know it was the voice of God?" Tony asked, incredulous.

Pia seemed miffed by the question. Like, *duh*. "Because it made me feel loved. It made me feel like loving back."

"You can't just take the parts of a religion you like," Tony insisted, kind of missing the point.

"Why not? All the editors of the Bible sure did, hiding whole Gospels in Egypt, completely changing stories in translations. Every church takes what serves it and spits the rest back in God's face. The Bible might contain the word of God, but don't forget it was written by people."

She had Tony there, so we all headed back to Phoenix to pick up the caravan—an old Chevy Luv truck with a Gypsy-style wooden canopy painted red, purple, and gold. Flowers covered the front, snake charmers and weird mythological birds graced either side, and a turbaned fortune-teller peered out from the back. Tony converted the thing to run on grease, and Magdelena added a crucifixion scene to the murals.

We traveled north in the two cars, then east through Idaho and Wyoming to Minneapolis, then toward New York by way of Madison, Chicago, and Detroit. We looped around the East Coast for a few months before heading up to Canada, getting a little attention in zines and local newspapers along the way.

Tony played around with themes and plots for the show. Magdelena, Pia, and I threw in our two cents here and there, but Tony seemed to have some unknowable vision he couldn't quite put his finger on. He'd spiral through different mythologies, trying a Hindu theme here, a Buddhist motif there, but he kept circling back to Christianity. "Damn Catholics," he said. "Never did a thing for people of color, but boy did they burn their imagery into our brains. You go to Oakland, you go to New Orleans, you go to the poorest village in Oaxaca or Sicily, and you got black people handing over their hard-earned money to some pervert priest preaching in some castle of a church. The faithful go home to their tenement hovels, thinking of some white Jesus and feeling like *they're* the ones who've sinned." He sparked up a joint, stared off at some far point on the horizon.

"Don't worry about it," Magdelena said. "Don't you *get* that we're satirizing the church? When Pia and I play virgin and whore onstage, you think we're promoting some papist agenda? Satire is what's bringing those bastards *down*."

I guess we never brought the bastards down, exactly, but as we inched back and forth across the country, old sins came back to haunt the diocese from Boston to Portland, and the priests wouldn't say their Hail Marys, and the bishops didn't want to admit mea culpa, and the church seemed to be doing a pretty good job digging its own grave for the feminists and the punks to dance on.

We performed.

Three years into our wayward journey, someone from a campus theater group in Yellow Springs, Ohio, called on Tony's prepaid cell phone and invited us to do a few shows. We'd just braved a small but scary crowd of angry-saved "God Hates Fags" protestors outside Kansas City. Dead of winter. The theater group offered us $2,500 but couldn't understand why we refused to do more than one performance a day. In the end, they accepted our terms, agreed to put us up for three days to do the three shows.

Barbaro sat in the front row, quiet-mesmerized.

Our last night on campus, he approached the cafeteria table where I sat with Madre, scarfing down a plateful of fried zucchini and drinking hot cider. He wore Carhart work pants and an old Ramones T-shirt. "It would please me greatly if I could spit fire for you," he said. "But I am not permissed to do so inside."

"What?"

His features reminded me of some prehistoric bird, nose curved, Adam's apple pronounced, eyes deep chocolate colored and hopeful. He cleared his throat. "You have performed for my colleagues and I beautifully. Now, if you will permiss me, I would very much like to reciprocate. The only inconvenience is that you will have to come outside."

Madre frowned, skeptical, but I tugged at her habit sleeve. "C'mon. We can finish our cider later."

"You will not be disappointed," Barbaro promised.

We left our steaming cups on the table, followed the stranger outside.

Under the three-quarter moon, he lit a torch. Madre and I huddled together against the January night as Barbaro gargled his lamp oil. He gestured for us to stand back, and we took a full step away before he exhaled his plume of fire.

Madre gasped.

I pulled her close to me as Barbaro let out a strange sound like an overused espresso machine. Flames poured from his nostrils.

"Where'd you learn to do that?"

He didn't answer. "I read about your road show when I was still training to become a doctor in Italia, before I gave up medicine for drama. As soon as I came here to Ohio, I implored the theater group to locate your brigade. I believe I have what it takes to be a fellow traveler."

I didn't know quite what to say. His fire-breathing was impressive, to be sure, but I'd never had anyone audition for me point-blank like that. I looked at Madre.

She spoke slowly. "We would, of course, have to consult the others."

"Yes, yes, of course." Barbaro nodded.

"Can you perform for them?"

"Certainly."

Magdelena and Tony had already retired to their cozy dorm rooms, didn't want to be bothered with a sad star-struck Italian outside in the quad, but Madre managed to lure Magdelena to the late-night audition and I convinced Tony, saying, "It's only polite. These people paid us really well and this guy's the one who got them to do it."

Tony couldn't argue with me on that one. Most nights, we'd be lucky to bring in a hundred bucks between the four of us. We were walking away from Antioch well fed and well rested, with $500 each and another $500 for the troupe's purse. Tony kicked back the comforter. "This better be banana-split-good," he mumbled.

Outside, it had started to snow. Barbaro's short dark hair looked almost gray under the flakes. "I do not want to presume," he said as he lit his torch, "but I must tell you, ever since I read of your *Death & Resurrection Show,* I knew I should be a part of it. In so many ways, I was born to spit fire for you."

The four of us stood in a semicircle as he gargled his lamp oil.

The snow fell from a black sky like weightless diamonds, and all at once—the wind roar—flames licked through the flurry.

Tony watched, captivated.

"He's a fairy tale dragon," Magdelena whispered.

We'd already planned a three-week break at a friend's house outside Miami, told Barbaro as much, and in the morning we headed south where everything smelled of cut grass and the winter sun tinged our skin brown.

Our last day on the beach, the bird boy Barbaro showed up with his red and white canvas backpack. The sight of him made my heart flutter inexplicably. I looked down at his red Converse high-tops, wondered if he was gay, decided he wasn't. "I hope you have not changed your minds about me," he said, tilting his head to the side.

Barbaro the great fire-spitter all the way from Venice, Italy. Of course we hadn't changed our minds. So we all piled into the hatchback and the caravan and headed toward Austin, motel by motel.

Turned out it would be a year for expansion. Come springtime, we found Lupe and the baby in a tiny adobe outside Albuquerque. Tony wanted to stop, drawn in by the ornate silver and blue Psychic Reader sandwich board propped between two desert shrubs.

Lupe stood at the door in fake leather pants and a white tank top, split lip, eye blackened, her dark hair a mess. Unashamed, she invited us in, spoke in lilting Spanglish. We drank lukewarm coffee at her wooden table, and for seven dollars, she promised Tony trouble in love.

"What can I do to avoid it?" he asked.

She shook her head. "No mucho."

Tony thought about that, lit a cigarette. He was smoking these super-skinny Capri Ultra Lights because he thought they'd help him quit. Instead he just looked like a milksop.

"What about you?" he asked, starring at Lupe. She had a little bit of a mustache over her full lips. "What's your destiny?"

Lupe gestured a quick circle around her darkened house. "Ese."

From the gleam in Tony's eyes, I could have predicted his next words. "I'll tell you what," he said. "You can keep the seven dollars, but I'll be the one telling your fortune today. You're about to change your destiny. You won't come with us right now. You have some business you need to take care of. But within twenty-four hours—forty-eight hours tops—something inside of you is gonna click. You'll come on the road with us. We've got a sideshow going. You can tell fortunes."

Lupe smiled, shook her head. "You're a sweet boy," she said. "*Simpático*. This is the thing that will bring you trouble."

Tony shrugged. "We're performing tonight over at the Outpost. Tomorrow in Cerrillos. The Circus House. Invitation's open."

Three days later we're all sitting at this cheesy artsy café in Taos, blurry orange and pastel desert landscapes on the walls, and in walks Lupe in a milk-stained blue T-shirt, baby on her hip. She'd brushed her hair, braided it.

"Took you long enough," Tony laughed.

Magdelena glared at him.

We'd all recently agreed not to invite performers on board without consulting the group, but even Tony hadn't honestly expected Lupe to show up. And with a baby?

"You have *got* to be kidding," Madre mumbled.

But what were we going to tell a bruised and nursing mother in an artsy café in the high desert mountains? Go home? She'd brought her own car, after all.

As Lupe ordered her espresso and cookies from the bar, Magdelena seethed: "I hope you don't think she's getting a share of our ticket sales. We're already splitting this five ways."

Lupe pulled up a chair, her biceps impressive for such a little woman. "I'll charge for my fortune-telling on the side if that's all right," she said. "I don't expect any part of your profits."

"What happened to the Me No Speak Good English?" I asked.

She blushed. "Makes people take their fortunes more seriously if they think they've got an exotic source. I'm actually from Indiana."

Magdelena rolled her eyes, but Lupe and the baby would make inroads to our hearts before we'd even crossed the Colorado border. Just another virgin mother: charming, charming.

She told fortunes on the side, nursed her baby into a fat toddler, inched her way into the show. With her strong arms, she became Magdelena's favorite catcher as we daydreamed all the way to the Canadian border and back again, headlights piercing the fog. Her only request: that we not return to Albuquerque. *Fair enough.* We'd never been able to draw much of a crowd there, anyway.

We washed through Nashville, songs of unrequited love, then crawled toward Pittsburgh, our route dictated by whims and rumors, anarchist houses promising a patch of love where we could roll out our sleeping bags, and paid gigs Tony managed to drum up on his prepaid cell phone. He'd find a new theater in Vermont willing to do promo or a festival in Olympia offering $100 an act, and we'd head off, hoping to rustle up something like a living.

The autumn we spent three weeks in Baltimore, my fellow travelers had been dropping like bug-sprayed flies into love. Tony and Lupe had started using words like *forever*. Magdelena had us driving hundreds of miles out of our way, linking even the most unlikely cities on routes that would take us through Chicago, so spent was she on an art institute student who moonlighted as a café manager. When she couldn't possibly justify a trip—no logic can take you from Orlando to New Orleans by way of Chicago—her lover would fly down for a weekend or even a morning. Barbaro had taken up with a busty French journalist who'd been stalking us for a magazine story. I checked out my own cleavage in the bathroom mirror. Unexpected jealousy. Even Madre Pia had started going googly for our young host, a fledgling filmmaker who wowed her with a tour of all the alleys, yards, and storefronts featured in John Waters movies.

I spent days browsing the shelves at Atomic Books, my evenings breathing boredom. There's nothing so tedious as love when you're not in it.

Paula happened to be renting a room in our filmmaker-host's wood-paneled row house. She drew pencil portraits of us all at the round breakfast table, sang in the shower at odd hours. Six feet tall with a full auburn beard, but there was something distinctly feminine in Paula's fine features.

It was a Tuesday night when I offered to take her out for a beer.

"Don't drink beer," she said. "But I'll have a shot or two of whiskey."

Nineteen years old, so we had to go to half a dozen places before we found a bartender who wouldn't card her.

In the green-lit booth at Frazier's on the Avenue, she ordered three shots of Jack Daniel's.

She'd been raised in some fundamentalist church, she told me, but since she grew out her beard and rejected the family religion, her parents and brothers acted as if she'd never existed.

"That's intense," I said.

But she just looked up at the ceiling, then smiled, resigned. "It's all right."

I tried to imagine Paula without her beard, going through the rites in some strict church. I said, "You must have been the star of the choir, with that voice."

She shook her head. "They didn't allow singing."

No singing? But she wanted to change the subject, wanted to know all about our travels. Had we been to New York City?

"Sure," I said. "ABC No Rio on Rivington Street."

"I've never left Baltimore," she admitted, then frowned, scratched her beard, took it back. "Actually, I went to D.C. once. On a field trip. We saw the Washington Monument. We were supposed to tour the White House, but the place was locked down. Some rabid environmentalist had fired shots over the fence. Anyway. Some beautiful hills between here and there."

Paula's confession filled me with a sudden panic that manifested itself as a series of physical reactions and faraway images: a tightening across my chest, the warmth of an unexpected neon-lit diner on a dusty highway; three quick breaths, crisp white sheets smoothed over a motel mattress; a fluttering behind my nose like a tiny bird trapped in my skull, gas tank on empty and no sign of life between here and the horizon.

It's not like I think the road is the greatest place on earth. It is not. It's always too hot or too cold, cramped quarters and salty greasy roadside food. Good coffee is shockingly hard to come by. Performance profits dwindle and rise pathetic-random. Americans are fat, talk wacky politics. Half the time the only radio stations you can get play damnation sermons or eighties cock rock. Strip malls and billboards selling junk you couldn't pay me to buy blanket the country. But the skull bird, she wants out.

I said, "Paula, Baltimore's cool, but there's no way in hell you were born to die here. Let us give you a ride out of town when we go. I can't say this road show has what you need, but it's a ride and I bet that's the best offer you'll get all year."

At month's end, when Magdelena found her new love in the shower with our young host and heartbreak rolled through that wood-paneled row house like a wrecking ball and Tony had to scramble to book us a string of shows heading north and west away from the tears and all-night drunken processing sessions, Paula followed us out to the curb, her life packed in a brown paper grocery bag. "Did you really mean it? About the ride?"

Tony's idea, I think, was that troupe performers would come and go, but from the beginning there was something magnetic about our little road show. It didn't draw very many people in, but those of us it drew, it held.

I myself never imagined being on the road with Tony and Magdelena for more than a season or two. I had fantasies of finding some beautiful seaside town to settle into, of meeting some green-eyed stranger who'd sweep me off my feet. Then I thought, *Well, maybe give it a year, then think about getting a real job.* It wasn't until the sunrise on Highway 84 rolling into Oregon last month that it dawned on me: This show had been my life for seven years. I had to pull over on the narrow desert shoulder. Barbaro slept in the backseat. Paula snored from the passenger's side. And that crazy rising cantaloupe sun behind us. *Seven years.*

═══ † ═══

"Your stigmata is so realistic," Judy says.

It's just the two of us now, saltwater lapping at our toes. I managed to slip away from the group interview at the Pig 'N Pancake, but not before agreeing to meet Judy later. She had a few questions for me, she said. She caught up with me at Clatsop Beach where the old shipwreck rests rusty-tired and half submerged and the sand glows a strange iridescent purple under the clouded sky.

"Isn't this lavender sand cool?" Judy says.

I nod. "I think it's radioactive—there was a nuclear power station upriver."

"Oh." She looks down at her bare feet, like maybe she should put her boots back on.

We sit on a spindrift log and she starts in. "So, are you Catholic?"

"Yeah," I say. "Raised Catholic."

"Oh. Whereabouts?"

I don't want to answer that. I'm from the place where you stand on what you think is ground and then they pull it out from under you like a cheap IKEA rug. Infrastructure of dreams and the hum of neon lights. "San Francisco," I finally say. "That area."

"Well." Judy sighs. "As I was saying. Your stigmata. It's rather eerie."

"I know. It's a weird trick. I've been trying to figure out how to pull a rabbit out of a hat or something, you know, more normal." I dig my heel into the wet sand.

Judy laughs uneasily. "Your 'trick' as you call it —how do you do it?" She leans in, like this is just between the two of us.

I can't help but laugh. "A magician never gives away her tricks."

She nods like Barbara Walters. "Is that what you are, Frankka? A magician?"

I could do without Judy and her stupid interview questions, but every time I think to tell her to shove it, I remember my fellow travelers at the Worker's Bar, spinning excited over the *L.A. Times. Grin through it, Frankka.*

"Maybe you can tell me a little something about your relationship with Christ," Judy tries.

The tide's coming in. These questions can't last forever, can they? We're performing tonight in Lincoln City. "I just enjoy being on the road," I tell her. "I've been lucky enough to hook up with some really talented people. My trick isn't anything special. The other performers just keep me around because they're used to me and I can drive for twenty-four hours before I start seeing elephants on the highway."

There's a silence. Judy's dark eyes keep wandering from mine to my hands, like she's hoping to catch a quick glimpse of my palms, but I've long since learned how to gesture and clasp without revealing my tiny pink scars.

"Some people," Judy finally says. "Some people would consider you the star of the show."

I shake my head again. "Magdelena and Madre are the stars, and probably better at this whole interview thing than me. I'm sorry."

"Don't be sorry," Judy says. Her teeth could be an ad for Crest White Strips. "I find you quite compelling." She stares at the rusted ship. "I wonder why they don't have that ship carcass hauled off the beach."

"I guess some people think it's beautiful." Looks like rain again.

"Do you believe in God?" Judy wants to know, but mercifully her cell phone rings.

Beep beep beep beep beep beep.

"Judy here . . . All righty . . . Well . . . Okay. Keep me posted."

Beep.

"No progress either way on the fires," she says.

"Seems like a strange job. Always waiting around for tragedy."

She shoots me a look like *You're calling my job weird?* then clears her throat. "I don't want to put you on the spot," she says.

I take this to mean that she fully intends to put me on the spot.

"I want you to tell me the truth, Frankka. Your bleeding, it's the real McCoy, isn't it?"

I laugh, secretly praying some faraway tragedy will suddenly make Judy's cell phone ring. "I didn't realize it was so convincing."

"Is that a yes or a no?" she insists.

I shake my head no, change the subject. "We've been in and out of L.A. twenty times. I'm sure Tony sent press releases. Why are you writing this story? Why this time?"

Judy smiles an ungodly smile, showing off her bleached teeth, says only, "Jesus is really big right now."

Brigid of Ireland
(IF YOU NEED A BEER)

A.K.A. Brigid of Kildare, Mary of Gael
FEAST DAY: February 1
SYMBOLS: a white cow, a candle

When Saint Brigid comes to me, she wears a simple apron, wipes her hands before she greets me. Ruddy-cheeked Irish hostess.

Some histories claim that Brigid was made a bishop "by mistake." The truth? Those sixth-century Celtic Christians were never as hung up as the Romans about a woman and her power. Female-headed abbeys were common as springtime. Women preached, heard confessions, even performed mass.

"Mistake" means "Don't tell Dad back in Rome how we're running the show up here."

"Mistake" is what they called kids like Brigid, born to unmarried parents, half princess and half slave.

Her chieftain father claimed paternity right off but said that until she got older she should live with her mom—a Christian woman he'd unceremoniously sold to a Druid priest before the baby was even born.

Brigid spent her childhood working on the Druid's farm and helping her mother run the household. But as soon as she hit adolescence, Chieftain Duffy showed up to claim custody.

Brigid packed her few things and moved in with Dad, but within a week he was already annoyed with his offspring. For one thing, he could do without her "Christian Charity," which amounted to giving all of his stuff away. Silver sets and groceries went to the poor family down the street. Horses were led away by beggars. Even the clothes in his closet went to the poor. "They need them more than we do," Brigid explained. But Duffy hardly considered himself the Goodwill. "Enough is enough, and I'm selling you to a king!" he fumed. He threw his daughter into his chariot and drove furiously to the castle.

Now, Duffy didn't want to appear too aggressive in front of the king, so he left his sword outside with Brigid when he headed in to strike the deal. Dumb move. Here comes a poor leper begging change. Brigid didn't have any money, so she offered him the sword.

When Duffy came out and discovered what she'd done, he lost it—started beating Brigid with his bare hands.

The king, who'd come down to meet his new bride, wrestled Duffy to the ground, questioned Brigid. "Why did you give your father's sword away?"

She brushed herself off. "Because the beggar needed it more than we did," she explained. "I'll gladly give away all that you have, too."

The king diplomatically broke off the engagement. *Thanks but no thanks.*

"My mother's fallen sick," Brigid told her still-livid father on their way home. "I'd like to go and take care of her. I'll run the Druid's dairy."

Good riddance, Duffy thought. "Go on, then. Until I find you a suitable husband."

At the dairy, Brigid resumed her habit of giving everything away. The Druid, less than pleased with the new management style, decided to confront her. After she'd handed out all the butter one morning, he demanded that she fill a large container for him.

Brigid said a quick abundance prayer and, miraculously, the vessel was full.

Impressed—but still pretty sure that the dairy would never turn a profit with this girl around—the Druid granted Brigid's request to release her mother from slavery.

Back at Duffy's house, new marriage plans were under way. This time her father had found a poet, but Brigid already knew that she wouldn't be any man's property—not even a poet's. She found a willing wife for the groom, then took the veil as a nun, later founding Kildare, the Church of the Oaks, a coed spiritual community that doubled as a school.

Quite the hottie by all accounts, Brigid wore a red-purple cloak over her habit, invoked her namesake, the Celtic goddess of inspiration and poetry.

"What's heaven like, Brigid?"

"It's a giant lake of beer! Everyone's welcome to come dip their mug, and we'll drink for all eternity."

The nuns and monks at Kildare ate simply—bread, milk, homegrown vegetables, the occasional fish—but guests were treated to huge feasts fit for the Lord himself. "Pull up a chair."

Irish hostess extraordinaire, my girl Brigid could turn water into ale and stone into salt. She presides over all transformations—birth and brewing, metalsmithing and poetry, the passage from winter to spring.

If you find yourself in need of a cold beer, just pray to Brigid, patron saint of travelers, poets, and bastard children. To protect your house from fire, weave wheat stalks into an X-shaped cross and hang it from the rafters. God granted Brigid everything she requested, and at once. But don't forget to end your prayer—all prayers—by saying "or whatever is best for all creatures in all realms." Sometimes what we want isn't what's best for all. To honor Brigid, leave a loaf of bread and an ear of corn on the windowsill on the eve of her feast, commune with oaks, and if anyone tries to enslave you, just start giving their stuff away.

I want to be a good hostess, Brigid, really I do. But Judy just will not get into her forest green Volkswagen Jetta and go away. She sits through our show at Theatre West in Lincoln City, cell phone in hand, refusing to give up on her merging forest fires. She follows us across the highway to watch us feast on black bean tacos and gulp down dark beer. She picks at her Mexican salad, complains about the shredded cheese. Enough is enough and I'm ready to sell her to a king, but the others want to go out for whiskey and vodka crans.

"Unwind to some country music?" Paula offers.

I shake my head no.

"I'll bunk with you tonight, okay?" Magdelena calls after me as I leave them all to their reporter.

"Sure." A few stars flicker in the night sky.

For some reason my palms ache. We've got tomorrow off, thank God. Then Monday in Sacramento, Tuesday in San Francisco, Wednesday and Thursday off, Friday in L.A. What if Judy follows us all the way down the coast? Surely she's got better things to do.

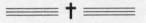

Alone in the blue motel room, I light a beeswax candle. The coiled waves of Clatsop Beach still crash in the back of my mind. The passing trucks sound like breakers on the shore. I close my eyes, and all of a sudden I'm being interrogated, everything sepia tinted and strange. It dawns on me where I am, and why: This is a trial, and I am the witch. I wake gasping.

Magdelena and Judy sit smoking at the table, mascara smeared, probably drunk.

"What are you doing here?" *This is a nonsmoking room.*

"Remember I told you I was gonna bunk with you?" Magdelena says softly. "Sorry we woke you."

Of course I meant *What's Judy doing here?* but as the dream fades into blue motel room, I realize the question's rude. "Sorry. I just had a weird dream." I climb out of bed, grab a plastic cup, and fill it with tap water from the bathroom, fuzzy headed.

"I'll be out of here in a flash," Judy promises.

"Good-night." I cover my head with the soft white pillow. *Please, Brigid, find Judy a new story.*

When I open my eyes again, the room is gilded with sunlight. Surely I'm dreaming all this gold. "It's beautiful," I whisper to no one.

Magdelena sleeps.

We've got a lot of driving ahead of us, but any day I can eat breakfast is a good day.

At the seaside café with my fellow travelers, I order blueberry pancakes and chicken-apple sausage, a double latte.

The waitress looks like Dianne Wiest, so I expect her to be all maternal love and wise wink, but she's grumpy as hell. "I guess some of us can eat carbs," she grumbles, looking me up and down. She scribbles my order on her pad and barks "B-cakes" to the Mexican cooks.

I look at Madre across the table. She wears a Catholic schoolgirl's uniform: white blouse, pleated skirt. I have a sharp sense of déjà vu. We've sat in this same café in exactly this same way. "We've been here before," I say.

Madre thinks about that for a long time, then shakes her head. "No," she says. "No, we haven't."

The waitress flings our plates on the table, unconcerned about who ordered what. We wait until she's turned her back to redistribute the breakfasts.

"What I wouldn't give to take Manny to the beach today," Lupe sighs. "Some time just to play."

"I can drive through the night," I offer.

Tony and Barbaro are game, but the others want to get a good start into California.

"It's, like, nine hours to the border," Magdelena insists.

I doubt that.

"Plus I have to bleach my hair." She pulls at her part to show off her creeping brunette roots.

"We can take the caravan," Paula offers. "Meet up in Sacramento tomorrow?"

That old truck with its painted wood canopy won't go over fifty, so it's a deal.

I lick the raspberry syrup from my fingers.

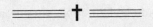

The warm sand on Sunset Beach feels like heaven under me. A dragon cloud floats past. Salty air. I watch Barbaro as he takes off for the shore.

After all his years of schooling to become a doctor, Barbaro had only practiced medicine for two years. "Sometimes it is right to battle death," he explained to me once. "But sometimes death has its reasons."

He'd lost a patient to what he'd only call "complications due to an error" and slumped into a heavy-hearted remorse. "It was truly an avoidable error," he said.

Three weeks after his death, the patient appeared to Barbaro in dream, thanked him for the error. The man's eyes gleamed with a joyous liberation Barbaro had never seen before.

The next morning, Barbaro traveled by train to the medieval hilltop village where the man had lived with his family. He waited in a dark café to spy on the man's wife and daughter. Late afternoon and he finally saw them: The women walked an easy, flowing walk through the piazza, as if a terrible burden had been lifted from their shoulders.

"I knew then that I had been drawn to medicine to heal souls, not bodies," Barbaro told me. "But medicine is not the thing that heals souls. Only drama can heal souls."

Only drama.

Tony builds gothic sand castles with Manny, croons love sounds at Lupe. They make a cute family, really. Lupe and the baby an anchor to Tony's wandering mind, he intentionally gentle when she expects the worst from men. She wears a turquoise bikini to show off the intricate octopus tattoo on the small of her back, but her scars are visible, too. Knife marks on her chest and back. Don't bother asking. "I've had a lot of fight in my life" is all she'll tell you.

I stretch out and let the sun wrap its tiger paws around me.

"The goddess Yemaya lives in those waves," Barbaro laughs, kicking up dry sand as he rushes up the beach toward me. He translates for a Catholic: "Our Lady of the Sea!" Every goddess in the world becomes a manifestation of Our Lady. I wonder if the Great Mother wept, back in the day, when she was demoted from known creator to mortal woman, mere mother of the male savior. Two thousand years is a slow climb back to glory. From mortal to saint, and then finally, just a few years ago, Vatican officials admitted that she ought to be called the Mother of God. Big words for guys who still considered all creation men's work, but who was God talking about in Genesis when God referred to God as Us? God might be one, but God's a couple, too, a team. I roll onto my belly, shade my eyes with my hand to get a good look at Barbaro. Probably Our Lady doesn't much mind what the Vatican calls her.

"You will come and bathe?" Barbaro wants to know. He's wearing these ridiculous pink Speedo trunks he must have gotten at a thrift store.

"Isn't it freezing?"

"You can try for just one minute?"

Manny comes running with a mischief-eyed smile, saltwater splashing out of his red bucket—he squeals as he drenches us both with the cold.

"Hey!" I scramble to my feet, go running for him.

"Mama! Help me!"

Now Barbaro's rushing back for the water. "Come on!" He's a silhouette against the sun.

My fellow travelers. "*Famiglia* from scratch," Barbaro calls us. Think of that. *Famiglia*.

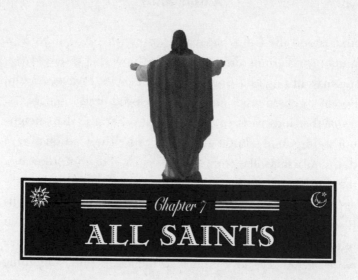

Chapter 7
ALL SAINTS

In school they called me "Lonely Only" because apparently no other Catholic girl ever lacked for siblings.

They called me "Freaky Frances" because toward the end of first grade someone decided that my eyes were set too far apart. *Who comes up with these decrees?*

"Her apartment's creepy!" the few kids I'd had over would bristle, but the apartment itself couldn't have given anyone the heebie-jeebies. My Nana, on the other hand, well, if you didn't know her, I guess my Nana could have been classified as creepy. Old even for a grandmother, she'd had my father late in life, believed his birth to be something of a miracle. Black clad and rosary mumbling, my Nana had only one beef with the Catholic Church: the Vatican II reforms of the late 1960s. "Exchange the peace before communion?" she'd mutter. "Liberal balderdash." Worse, the priests had all but forgotten their Latin. It's not like my grandmother ever really understood the Latin, but maybe that's why she'd liked it so much—mysterious and unknowable. Now they'd started saying mass in English. "English!" *What were we, Protestants?* Oh, how my grandmother grieved her beloved dead language.

Other kids went to All Saints K–8 because their neighborhood public schools sucked, because the Catholics gave out scholarships like communion wafers. They went because their mothers had something to prove to their fathers' mothers or because they'd gotten busted with a joint at DeAvila Elementary. They were Catholics, for the most part, but their religion seemed a lighter thing than ours, something they wore like an accessory pinned to their uniforms, something they could call themselves even if their parents were, quite frankly, more taken with the Dalai Lama than with any tired old cult of the male savior.

I imagined that in New York or Puerto Rico—Chicago, even—other girls had old-school, pope-fearing guardians like mine. I'd seen them in movies. But in California, my grandmother was a freak.

I longed for normal parents you could call by their first names. Second-generation Mexican immigrants or cool professionals who worked at religious nonprofits and thought Vatican II was "a step in the right direction." They'd show up at school in jeans or business suits, roll their eyes when the nuns weren't looking. Their apartments smelled of Nag Chaampa incense. Beads hung in their doorways. Potted plants dangled from ceiling hooks. Old Angela Davis posters in the kitchens, U2 records on the turntables. Or they lived in actual houses in the Sunset district, ate off Williams-Sonoma dishes. Better yet, a single mom with a job—an empty apartment where all the fly-children could gather after school, sneak sips of Bacardi and practice French-kissing each other's hands. I'd been invited to homes like those, mostly for birthday parties to which everyone but Ezekiel Goldstein got a pink-enveloped invitation. The kids didn't ostracize me the way they did Ezekiel Goldstein, that much I had to be thankful for. Poor little mop-haired kid, how he ever ended up at All Saints K–8 remained a mystery. Rumor had it his parents were in prison for organizing some mad political protest at Concord Naval Weapons Station. Foster care. The kids taunted him. "Jew boy!"

Here was something worse than just being white.

"Jew boy!"

Maybe if he'd made a joke out of it, shrugged it off, or bribed them with Cheetos, they could have accepted him, eventually, but Ezekiel Goldstein stood defiant under the monkey bars in his pressed blue slacks, yelling, "Jesus was a Jew!"

This, of course, was too much for the fly-children to handle, and they all swarmed to tattle to Sister Mehitable. "Ezekiel Goldstein took the Lord's name in vain!"

In my fantasies, I became one of the fly-children. I stuck up for Ezekiel Goldstein, saying, "He's right." Or at least, "Leave him alone." But what good would it have done for Freaky Frances to stand up to that mob united against the scrawny mop-haired boy alone on the playground? I had my own cross to bear.

Last bell, and all those spongy-mouthed kids buzzed into their little clusters, loosely grouped by race and age, to catch buses home or BART trains to Stonestown Mall or the Esprit outlet. "Don't you have anyone to walk home with, Freaky Frances?" they'd call after me. Or, "See ya later, Lonely Only!"

But truth told, I wasn't so lonely. When my classmates started circling into their little swarms after the initial social anarchy of kindergarten and first grade, the saints became my companions. They'd leap from their stained glass or stone statue perches in the chapel, follow me to the cafeteria to eat lunch with me at the far corner table. They'd walk me home, making me invisible to the tough fly-girls who wanted to pick fights, invulnerable to the pushers at the corner bus stop on Dolores. We'd walk, they in their weird flowing white or brown capes, me in my plaid skirt and starched white cotton blouse. We'd talk about this and that, life, all the crazy things they'd done in their youths, self-mortification and flinging themselves into tombs and whatnot, about what it would be like when I got my driver's license. They'd point out the different species of birds perched on flophouse rooftops, admire the healing herbs that forced themselves up through tiny cracks in the sidewalk.

To me, the saints weren't church people, exactly. We lit candles for them in cathedrals and shrines, sure, but the saints existed separate and alive from school rules or Father Michaels's Sunday admonitions. They required no confessions, didn't seem to believe in any kind of hell a girl couldn't claw her way out of. They'd leave me at the doorway to my apartment building, between the iron gate and the dirty red carpeted stairway leading up. "Until tomorrow, Frances Catherine!"

"See you tomorrow."

I hardly ever studied for religion class—couldn't quote scripture to save my life—but I impressed even pinch-faced Sister Mehitable with my vast knowledge of the saints, their wild maudlin lives, their miracles. Of course I knew the answers—my friends whispered them in my ear. Sometimes I had to edit their explanations to please the sisters, of course:

Why did the saints intentionally make themselves uncomfortable, sleeping on stone beds and pricking their fingers?

To better identify with Our Lord's suffering, I'd say.

But according to my saint friends, it was more complicated than that. Clare of Assisi, who wore a hair shirt under her rough Franciscan habit in that cruel Umbrian heat, told me it amounted to a kind of joy training. "If my happiness is so weak it can be destroyed by an itch, a mosquito, a foul wind, is it really happiness? The risen Christ taught us that we needn't ever let suffering have the last word." She cocked her head to the side, gazed upward. "Hungry, ill, and overworked," she said, "my joy is thick."

Sometime around the sixth grade, Ezekiel Goldstein got transferred to a secular school for geniuses. I did not say goodbye. Soon my classmates' taunts dwindled to the occasional "See ya, Freaky," and by the time eighth grade was winding down and we were all getting ready for high school, even the fly-girls with the very neatest cornrows or the biggest feathered do's had started getting caught in the bathroom with boys, sent to juvie, busted behind chapel with little plastic baggies of cocaine stolen from their now-divorced parents' glove compartments or film canisters of weed they'd bought on the panhandle. I learned to gossip, made a few friends—foreign exchange kids, mostly, and transfers who didn't seem to notice my eyes being so far apart. The saints didn't walk me home much anymore, but they still winked at me from their stained glass perches and tried to remind me in their quiet ways that there existed a world beyond All Saints K–8, a world that might just be shot through with something like grace.

Chapter 8

TRUST LIFE, SLEEP SOUNDLY

Madre Pia knows someone who knows someone. The long and short of it: She's gotten us booked at a Presbyterian church in Sacramento. We've never actually performed at a church before. *Will it feel any different?*

We cut over to Interstate 5 from Newport, drive half the night listening to Paul Simon on the tape player. High passes and winding asphalt gray from Grants Pass and over the Shasta range.

Tony, Lupe, and Manny sleep in a huddle in the backseat.

I keep my eyes on the yellow lines. "Do you still think you were born to spit fire for *The Death & Resurrection Show?*" I ask Barbaro. It's been a couple of years since that snowy winter night at Antioch.

He closes his eyes. When Paul Simon finishes singing about his one-trick pony, Barbaro nods. "This road show is my home."

Home. I can remember times when I said the same thing. This small circus we built together—my fellow travelers—all the people who had marked me in one way or another, who had loved me and I had loved. For years I believed in nothing more than the art and reverie that emanated from the very center of each of us and leapt forth onto the makeshift stage every night in our wild cabaret—the grand confrontation between reality and fiction in which fiction always won out. *When had things changed?*

I have the sudden urge to reach over, touch Barbaro's sun-kissed jaw line. His new buzz haircut makes him look like a featherless bird. I worry about his mouth—all that lamp oil, all those flames. "You never get tired of it?"

Barbaro laughs. "Of course I become tired. Home is a place you become tired of, but it is also a place that holds you. You can leave it if you like. Your family will miss you, but they will allow you to go without protest. They know, as you know, that you will return one day, and when you do, you will not be a stranger. This is the beauty of home."

"But none of us could leave the show. Or, if we did, we'd be replaced. The story would close in around the space we left."

Barbaro hums.

Here's what I love about Barbaro: his complete faith in the elegance of his destiny. This humble show.

He says, "Life sings to me beautifully."

I can't imagine that kind of contentment. I fret and worry intermittently, am tormented and distracted by doubts I can't even name. Wrong turns in life and so much time passing you might not be able to retrace your steps. I'm afraid of hurting people and afraid of not doing what I need to do for fear of hurting people. I wonder if I'll ever have children, wonder if it's even moral to bring children into this world of hunger and war—a world where those who want to leave a city under siege are told to go to a certain mosque and even those who go waving white flags are killed. I'm afraid my failure to get a college degree will one day catch up with me, a ghost on a desert highway. I worry that my wondering faith isn't good enough, that there'll be hell to pay at the end. I worry I'll never have sex again. I imagine what my life would be like if I'd stayed with the labor rights activist in Minneapolis who professed his undying love after just a few nights. I grieve because when Tony and I sold everything at that yard sale back in Santa Cruz, I imagined this life on the road—without a real job and the hours spent in crushing traffic to and from—would ultimately save me from all these worries. Live free and ramble, that was the idea. I say, "You trust life, Barbaro."

His eyes bright. "What reason has life given me not to trust it?"

That night in a second-floor Super 8 Motel suite in Red Bluff, California, I stare up at the dark ceiling. *What reason has life given me not to trust it?* I wonder if I'm some kind of incurable malcontent, forever ungrateful for all the beauty and good fortune life showers on me. In college, I went to see a therapist. The vacant-eyed woman with long black hair sat in her leather armchair and listened to my weekly monologues for nearly three months, then told me I couldn't trust anyone or anything because I'd never been able to heal from my parents' sudden death. Surely the sense of abandonment I felt after my favorite professor's suicide stung so deep because it opened old wounds: the four-year-old waiting at the window of her babysitter's apartment for the mother and father who promised not to be gone long, mint chip ice cream long since licked from plastic bowls and all the songs that babysitter knew sung and sung twice. I waited.

"You never had a chance to process that loss," the therapist told me. I don't even remember her name. She wore long brown skirts and button-up blouses, sat with rough hands folded in her lap. "I think it's quite interesting that your parents are buried right here in Santa Cruz, and yet you say you haven't been to visit their graves since your grandmother died."

Whatever. I'd processed that loss. Crying with my Nana in her golden armchair "What kind of God?" and "What kind of God?" until all the tears in this world were cried and my hunger welled up like an empty cave, the aching reminder that I was alive. Never had a chance to process it? I'd processed it, all right. I'd wept it, watered my grief, nurtured abandonment, dried it all off, prayed it undone, bled it out. No, this restless disquiet was something else.

Barbaro sleeps under the polyester bedspread, his back curled to me like the wall of a cave. I'm wearing a red silk camisole I stole from Magdelena, can only wear it nights when she's not around. I snuggle into Barbaro's warm skin. Maybe his dumb trust can lull me into sleep.

The Seven Sleepers

(IF YOU NEED REST)

A.K.A. The Seven Sleepers of Ephesus
FEAST DAY: July 27
SYMBOL: a dog

There were seven of them on trial that day in Ephesus. The charge: banned faith. Third-century Turkey and it was still a Pagan's world. The emperor Decius had come to town on his high horse, imposing his persecutory decrees against Christians. The men hid in their homes, fasting and praying, but they were quickly discovered.

The emperor offered a plea bargain. "Renounce your wacky beliefs and live, or persist in them and die."

The young men weren't given long to decide, but their choice was easy. They believed.

The hammer of justice. The death penalty. No opportunity for appeal. They had twenty-four hours.

They gave their money and property to the poor, kept only a few coins. With their loyal dog, they retreated to a cave on the rocky northern slopes of a nearby mountain to savor a last meal together and prepare to meet the maker they believed in so wholeheartedly. They ate their eggplant and pilaf, said a final prayer together, fell asleep on the dirt floor of their unhidden mountain refuge.

In the morning, the soldiers marched up the rugged face of the mountain with a mission, but when they found the seven sleeping, they decided not to waste the crucifixion nails. They just walled up the cave. Sentence carried out, faith contained. The seven slept, their loyal dog keeping guard like an angel just outside.

A Christian came by and wrote the martyrs' story on the outside of the cave. Years passed. Times changed. Two hundred—maybe three hundred years. The whole area had gone Christian, but the doctrine of bodily resurrection was a matter of hot debate.

Back on the mountain, a new landowner figured he'd take a pickax to that old wall, use the cave for his cattle. His masons started hacking away, but all the ruckus woke up the sleepy faithful. They rubbed their eyes, quickly hid in the depths of the cave, waited until the workers had gone.

Thinking it had only been a night, they were surprised how hungry they felt. Diomedes volunteered to go into town to pick up some breakfast. Maybe the soldiers were running late?

Ephesus appeared like a dream. Familiar, but built up in new places, crumbling where it had been new. Pastures he could have sworn were vacant had become libraries and markets. Crosses hung over gates and church doors. Homes he remembered from yesterday had fallen into disrepair. Diomedes was beyond confused. *What is this? Yesterday no one dared say "Jesus Christ," and now the crosses everywhere? Is this Ephesus?*

"Where'd you get these old coins?" the baker wanted to know when Diomedes pushed them across the counter.

Where, indeed?

When Diomedes finally got his bearings, he explained where he'd come from, and how. He led the bishop and the prefect to the believers' hideout, and their resurrection was celebrated with wine, fire, and dancing. When the party was over, the sleepers lay down in their cave-beds with their loyal dog and died for real.

The new Christian emperor wanted to build golden tombs, but the sleepers appeared to him in a dream, saying, "We don't want anything fancy. Just bury us in our cave. We can rest peacefully now."

Even death needn't have the last word.

The emperor had the cave adorned with precious stones, and a great church was built. Every year—to this day—revelers feast, toasting the sleepers' bodily resurrection, their simple trust.

Some say it's just a legend—no truth to it at all—but you can visit their tombs outside Ephesus any time you like, read the inscription on the stone wall, see for yourself.

If you toss and turn at night, kept awake by worry and doubt, just build an altar to the seven sleepers, patrons of insomniacs. Light a magenta candle, close your eyes, and repeat like a mantra: "I am dreaming the universe into the future." Everything changes in good time.

Chapter 9

GOD HATES SINNERS

"Jeez—something else must be going on at the church," Lupe says as we round the corner. Cars are double-parked on both sides of the street. A mass of sunburned and vitamin-starved bodies sway under the valley sun in front of the tall steeple. "Maybe turn down there?" She points, hopeful.

The baby sings along with Santana on the radio.

"Oh, there's always some shit going on in Sacramento," Tony says. "Some rally or something. I wonder if the show got listed anywhere."

I graze the bumper of a Lexus trying to fit the hatchback into a tiny parking place in front of a Chinese restaurant six blocks from the church.

"Not the Lexus!" Tony laughs.

"Moooo-shu shrimp," Manny cries when he sees the restaurant's red lanterns. "I want moo-shu!"

Lupe nods in my rearview mirror. "Chinese sounds good." She's always agreeing with her baby, more to make sure he gets his way than for any shared taste in food.

"Right on. I'll meet you guys over at the church?"

"We will bring for you a doggie bag," Barbaro promises.

The streets are packed with muscle men in white T-shirts and mothers holding half-naked children. An afternoon concert, maybe. A peace protest or a war protest. On the corner, a legless man in a wheelchair holds a hand-painted sign: "God Hates Sinners."

Weird. We've never been picketed in California before, and this crowd's way too big for just us. Maybe the Presbies have come out as pro-choice. *Are they pro-choice?* Presbyterians. I can't remember.

"Christ died for your sins!" someone yells as I approach the church square like a lost tourist.

Green and purple tents are pitched on the sidewalk.

"Praise be to God!"

There's a woman carrying a cooler and a book bag. "Pabst Blue Ribbon, one dollar! Bibles, fifty cents!"

I feel disoriented, the sun an iron gate on my back, the crowd like a misplaced county fair without any rides.

Old men and children kneel in a circle, praying. "God forgive us our sins . . ."

Then a shrill voice from behind me, "That's her!"

"Hey!"

"Saint Cat!"

"Praise God!"

As I turn, a throng of heavy women moves toward me like a giant sea creature.

A banner waves from a bald man's bicycle: "1 Cross, 2 Nails, 4 Given."

Then a banshee shriek: "It's the blood girl!"

"Blasphemer!"

Sudden panic. Everything in surreal slow motion, blur of blues and reds. More crowd moves toward me from the side. Open air, but I feel claustrophobic.

"Frances Catherine!"

A dozen hands reach for me at once—white, brown, and black; dirty, scratched, and calloused. "Frances Catherine!"

A little boy with skinned knees cries, caught up in the commotion unprepared. "Mama?" he sobs.

I want to dive under something, but what? I turn to run, but only more bodies closing in on me. Arms outstretched, mouths open and twisted, gawking. They're yelling something, but it all sounds like a tape player running on dying batteries, low and distorted. Blur of humanity and not one familiar face. My heart races and all I can think is, *They're going to crush me.* I want to scream, open my mouth, but nothing comes. The ground cracks under me.

"Frances Catherine!" A body heavy on my back. I start to fall forward.

God, help me.

A hand grabs me by the wrist, I trip, inhale quickly, about to be trampled, but the hand pulls me to my feet. "Come on, Frankka."

Is it Paula's voice?

She yanks me between two sweaty bodies, in through a heavy door. She manages to pull it closed before the horde can swarm in behind us. All quiet. Dark cool cement floor hallway.

"Are you all right?" Paula wants to know.

"What the hell's going on?"

She doesn't answer me, leads me through the dim cold hall into a windowless room. Magdelena and Madre sit silent at a giant oak desk. They look up as we enter, but no trace of emotion crosses their pale faces.

"Will someone please tell me what's going on?"

Paula speaks slowly. "The story—it came out this morning in the *L.A. Times.*"

"And? L.A.'s five hundred miles from here."

Paula places her hand on my shoulder.

Madre Pia clears her throat. She's wearing a white jumpsuit that makes her look like a big bunny. No makeup. Freckled nose. "It's not as bad as it seems," she says.

I take this to mean that it—whatever it is, exactly—is even worse than it seems.

"I—"

Paula pushes the newspaper across the oak desk. It takes me a full minute to register the bold headline:

MANIFESTING THE WOUNDS OF CHRIST
Hysterical Disorder or True Mystical Phenomena?

There's a quarter-page color picture of me onstage at the River Theater, eyes half open, arms outstretched, palms exposed and bleeding. Somehow the bright of the camera flash and the overhead spotlights conspire to create a halo over my crown of thorns. Then two insets: the publicity shot of the group and a close-up of my open hand against a white motel sheet. My scar. I feel nauseous.

My fellow travelers wait, silent.

I sit down, scan the text:

> While Frances Catherine skirts questions regarding the veracity
> of her wounds, an anonymous source within the performance
> troupe attests to their authenticity. A preliminary independent
> analysis of a blood sample obtained by the *Times* proved incon-
> clusive, but Dr. Deborah Pappas, a leading expert in stigmatic
> phenomena, characterized the data as compelling. "If this is a
> hoax," she said, "it is an extremely well-executed hoax."

The article goes on to list famous stigmatics throughout
history, to note that the wounds are more common in women
than in men, more common among priests and nuns than
among laypeople, and to quote professors of religious psy-
chology on hysterical hypochondria and other "scientifically
plausible" explanations.

Sinking in my wooden chair, I feel cold, heavy. If there
were anything in my stomach, I'd throw up.

"Are you okay?" Magdelena whispers.

A rage wells up from behind my gut. Everything is suddenly clear: the flash from the audience at the River Theater,
Judy in our blue motel room in Lincoln City, Magdelena
spinning at the Worker's Bar. My face flushes. "You fucking
bitch, Magdelena."

She gulps an inhale like I've punched her.

I have no sympathy. "I always knew you were a selfish
bitch, but this is unreal." I can taste the bile between my words.

Magdelena stares at me. She's wearing this little red dress
like she's on her way to a tango. Three-minute pause. She

stands up, stone-faced, lifts her black purse from the floor. The door clicks shut behind her.

Another thick slice of silence. I bury my face in my stupid scarred hands.

"I'm sure she didn't mean any harm," Madre offers.

The fluorescent lights flicker. I can still feel the sweaty bodies on my back. A surge of hot disgust. "Shut up, Pia. I bet you had a hand in this, too. The both of you so hell-bent on getting famous. Big circulation, huh? Well, welcome to hell. How do you think those 'God Hates Sinners' fundies are gonna like your drag queen ass?" I want to breathe, but I'm just shaking, spitting words. "Fuck you."

For a split second Pia looks like the fat boy on the playground who's just had his homemade valentine ripped to shreds and thrown in his face and I wish I could take it back, just that last fuck you, but I sit there, tight-jawed. *I have to get out of here.*

Paula follows me from the tiny room. "You need to calm down, Frankka," she says to my back. "You need some time to digest all of this."

I can hear my heart beating in its tiny chamber, the skull bird behind my eyes.

Then a child's voice from the stairwell. "Miss Frances?" The little girl stands in ripped jeans and a stained yellow T-shirt. "Miss Frances, my father is very sick and—"

"How did you get in here?" A scolding hand pulls the girl from behind. "Where are your parents?"

"I have to speak to Miss Frances," the girl insists.

A door opens and shuts.

Dim-lit hallway and church offices.

"I'm sorry about that." A slender middle-aged woman with short brown hair appears from the stairwell. She wears a light cotton suit, no makeup—the type you're not sure if she's a lesbian or a nun. "We weren't prepared for your security needs." Her tone is matter-of-fact. "Quite honestly, we didn't fully understand the content of your show when we agreed to let you use the church, but be that as it may. The police have just arrived." She sticks out her hand. "I'm Carol, the minister here. You must be Frances Catherine?"

I nod slowly, don't shake her hand. It's so strange to be called by my childhood name.

"We weren't prepared, either," Paula admits.

"Well," Carol says, "between the Sacramento Police Department and our community volunteers, we should be able to handle it. Of course, the phone has been ringing off the hook all morning. Everything from media inquiries to bomb threats, but I think we've got the building secured. By tonight we'll have a private security team."

I stand silent. Surely she's kidding if she thinks we'll still be here by tonight.

"The show must go on," Paula says dumbly.

Out of here is all I can think. I'm trapped in some Protestant nightmare. *Run away.* Carol is talking about something, blocking my escape. When she finally takes a half step to the left, I lunge for the door handle. *The hell out of here.* Push and run. The outside air is a kiln, but just a few dozen people mill around in the shade of an old oak. I take a deep breath. *Which way?* Then a siren shriek: "Frances Catherine!"

"She's over here!"

"God is great!"

The milling bodies suddenly swarm together. They're moving toward me, chanting something, but all I can hear is the fly-children from All Saints K–8 yelling, "Freaky Frances! Freaky Frances!" Hands grab me from behind and pull me back inside. "Frances," Carol scolds me.

A banging at the door.

"We've got to get her out of here," Paula says.

I am led down two flights of cement stairs to a musty basement full of pamphlets and canned food, giant white bags of rice. A metallic taste in my mouth.

"Don't think we never had to smuggle a draft dodger out of here," Carol says as she reaches into a cupboard and produces a green army flashlight. "Listen," she says. "The tunnel will get you about a half mile away to the old minister's basement. I've already called him. He's expecting you." She takes a business card from her suit pocket and hands it to me. "Call my cell when you're ready to come back. We'll have a better handle on the situation by then." She opens a small wooden door.

I hesitate at the threshold.

"Do you need me to take you?"

"No. I'll be okay."

Just a few paces in, the musty-damp tunnel narrows. I'm only five-foot-four, but I have to walk with my head bowed, shoulders rounded. Imagine a lanky draft dodger down here, hunched over, making his way between these walls, brave-scared.

I try to remind myself that anyone who was anyone in the ancient world had to make an initiatory descent, but it's dark down here.

A half mile, but who can gauge distance in the dark? My flashlight is an angel, illuminating round by round the brick and mortar path. What if an earthquake hit right now? What's to stop the earth's plates from shifting at this very moment? *Shut up, brain.* It's quiet down here. What's it like to be trapped underground? Buried? When I was a kid—maybe seven or eight—the winter rains came heavy after a drought, in sheets and torrents. Rivers flooded and cliffs turned into landslides from Mendocino to Monterey. On the TV news, a reporter stood in the gusting wind, knee-deep in mud, clinging to her microphone. A little house in Santa Cruz had been washed clear off the mountain and swallowed by the earth. Three children asleep in their shared double bed, missing. Search and rescue crews on the scene and the reporter talking about how maybe the kids are trapped in an air pocket underground. I lay wrapped in a wool blanket on the couch in our living room, listening to that wild pelting rain against the windows, watching the glowing screen for hours, and here's this sudden hope: The three kids are sleeping soundly and alive in their beautiful little air pocket. I imagined the pocket round, like a bubble, with smooth dark walls. The sky kept dumping on our apartment roof and on the reporter in her yellow rain-coat, pouring out of gutters and rushing to turn the mountains back to ocean. When even the reporter had to get out of the storm's way, I prayed to Our Lady of Perpetual Help to keep my three new stranger-friends safe in their little bed in their dark pocket. I must have fallen asleep before they found the bodies, because it was years before it occurred to me: There are no livable air bubbles under mudslides.

The tunnel angles to the right, seems to narrow again. It's hard to get a good breath down here. My chest feels tight. Maybe I should turn around. Maybe this is stupid. Maybe it's all a trick. Maybe they're going to keep me down here now, study me, stick me with pins. Maybe something in my blood will give them the proof they're looking for. Irrefutable evidence of—*What?*—God? God in my blood. The smell of wet dirt. I keep moving forward. *Breathe, Frankka.* The walls feel like they're closing in.

Click.

What is it?

Click.

Then a soft light. "You coming, kid?"

Chapter 10

QUICK PRAYER

Martín de Porres

(IF YOU NEED INVISIBILITY)

A.K.A. Martín of Charity

FEAST DAY: November 3

SYMBOLS: a broom, small animals, healing herbs

Martín de Porres, patron saint of social justice, please make the Jesus freaks blind to me.

When two escaped prisoners begged sanctuary in your monastery cell, you had them kneel and pray. When the cops showed up to search the place, they found no sign of the fugitives.

Martín, bastard child of a freed slave, you were apprenticed to become a barber-surgeon—not a bad prospect for a poor fatherless kid—but you wanted only to work for God. At the Dominican Friary of Rosario in Lima, you became a lay servant because the bigoted rules wouldn't allow you to call yourself a full brother. Black man. But you did your chores without resentment. Saint of the Broom. For nine years you swept and prayed, raised more than $2,000 a week for the poor. Nine years, and at last the racist rules went bent for you. You became a monk, a full brother! Your responsibilities included haircuts and health care. You grew herbs in your cell, healed the sick, founded an orphanage, a hospital, and a veterinary clinic.

When the monastery prior instructed you to set out poison for the mice, you did as you were told, but not without warning the rodents. You crept out into the yard, called your mice friends together, and offered them a deal. "Stay out of the buildings," you said. "I'll bring your snacks outside to you each night." And so you did. Mice and monks lived in harmony.

Oh, Martín, flying brother, you used to rise up in the air as you prayed, emanating supernatural rays of light. From your monastery cell, you appeared all over the world. Traveling merchants saw you in Central America, Mexico, Asia, and northern Africa. You counseled the sick, aided prisoners. You knew instantly where you were needed, healed with your touch, could enter and exit through locked doors without a key.

You even predicted the date of your own death.

Twenty-five years later, your casket was opened so your remains could be moved to a better tomb. The sweet smell of roses! Your body lay incorrupt. One friar secretly removed a rib, hid it under his habit, but immediately the bone radiated heat. That night in his cell, the heat became so intense that the friar decided to confess and surrender the bone. He kept just a fragment, but the fragment emanated just as much heat, and soon he was forced to confess again and surrender what he had taken.

Oh, Martín, Scorpio boy, you had no fear of darkness. But I'm afraid. The Jesus freaks—they scare me. When they close their eyes, what God do they see? When they kneel and pray, do they also rise? Do they envision themselves undercover agents for social justice and transformation, as you did? Why then the frenzied hatred? Why the threats of damnation? Why the obsession with sin? Why the reaching hands? Oh, Martín, make them blind to me.

Chapter 11

REFUGE

"Been a helluva long time since anybody came through this way," the old minister chuckles as I step over the threshold into his basement. He's got a white beard, alcohol-rosy cheeks.

I follow him past shelves of boxes and books, old papers and broken radios, up unfinished wood stairs, through a laundry room, and into a bright yellow tiled kitchen. The glare of refuge.

When the old minister smiles, he looks like some elfin folk singer. "Read all aboutcha," he says, smacking his lips. "Fellow who works over at the food closet brought the newspaper. Big story, huh? *Whoo-eee.*"

I shrug, trying to look blasé, but surely my humiliation is obvious.

"Y'hungry?" He rubs his hands together.

"Starving," I admit.

At a butcher block table, the old minister cuts thick slices of white bread, Monterey jack cheese, Italian salami.

It's been years since I let red meat pass my lips, but a girl should eat what she's served.

He sets the sandwich in front of me on a chipped yellow plate, sits down across from me, and rubs his beard. "Bourbon?"

"Sure."

He pours two good-sized glasses of Rebel Yell, knocks his own back like it's water. His white cotton undershirt is sweat stained and dirt streaked.

I feel disoriented, weirdly shy without my troupe, feet cold in my boots. I chew on my bread and salty-dry meat. "Aren't you going to ask me about my hysterical hypochondria?"

He laughs. "Damned if I care about *that*." He leans back in his chair, stretches his thick legs. "Listen, kid, I've got a tree to plant. Make yerself at home."

Home. The concept seems foreign. I watch through the uncurtained window as the old minister works under the mean Sacramento sun, forcing his shovel into the earth. The potted lemon tree behind him droops slightly to one side, looks like it could use the new rooting ground. Imagine that—having a piece of earth to sink your toes into, to hang onto.

The bourbon creeps down my throat and into my bloodstream like a poison, like an elixir. This bright kitchen seems states away from the pulsing mob back at the church. I trace the periphery of a tile on the wall, try to tell myself I overreacted, that maybe that heavy crowd wasn't so scary after all, but when I close my eyes, all I can see are those reaching hands, the bodies closing in on me. I finish my drink, take another bite of my sandwich, but it's useless. I can't get the taste of betrayal out of my mouth. Metallic.

What if our characters aren't measured by the way we live day-to-day? What if we're judged instead at moments like these, angry and running? My jaw tightens.

The old minister steps back inside, wiping sweat from his forehead with a cloth handkerchief, and I try to imagine him as a young minister: dark hair, clean shaven, earnest-faithful. He sits down at the butcher block table to roll himself a ciga-rette from a large blue can of tobacco. "You headin' back for your show pretty soon?"

"I can't," I admit. "I'm not hungry anymore."

He nods, doesn't seem to need any further explanation. His clear blue eyes remind me of someone, but I'm not sure who. "Well," he says, licking his cigarette closed and lighting it with a wooden match. "You sure got those ticket sales boom-ing, eh?" He shakes his head. "Got the new ministers over there thinkin' they've been in the wrong business all these years—*whoo-ee.*" The telephone rings an old-fashioned ring. He picks up the corded receiver.

"Yep? . . . Naw . . . Yeah, she was through here 'bout an hour ago, but she didn't linger. Said she was headin' out to Stockton . . . Uh-huh . . . Sure . . . No trouble."

He replaces the receiver, winks at me. "Stockton. That'll throw 'em."

A blue wave of exhaustion crests over me.

"But listen, kid, don't you worry a damn 'bout all those people. They'll be on to somethin' else by next week—ferget all aboutcha. 'Til then you can hide out here if ya like, do whatcha want. Guest room's thataway." He points toward the hall.

"Thanks," I say. The bourbon is sloshing around in my head, disinfecting things. "I wouldn't mind a nap."

★   ★   ★

In the single guest bed, I dream of lightless tunnels. I'm pulling a red wagon full of peaches down a long highway at night. It's raining. An elephant lumbers along up ahead. On either side of the road, human hearts hang like fruit from trees, weighing down orchards. Then a bright room. Magdelena. The reporter is beating her with a heavy broomstick, trying to kill her. "What are you doing?" But Magdelena is already dead. Judy covers her with a sheet, turns to me, and says, "You're an accomplice now." I'm confused, but when the reporter leaves and Magdelena turns and moans under the sheet, I panic. I want her dead, too. *Where's the broomstick?*

When I open my eyes it's dark. *What motel is this?*

I creep down the soft carpeted hallway toward the flickering light of a television screen.

The old minister sits on a wine-colored couch watching the news, a plate of green beans and meat loaf in his lap. He doesn't acknowledge me when I sit down next to him.

Onscreen, a blindfolded hostage dressed in orange pleads for his life. Young men in white, eyes ablaze with the horror of survival, rush bloodied bodies on stretchers through dusty streets. Women in black chase them, weeping and reaching, their faces half covered. A wrecked car. A maimed child. A burned-out building. The newscaster wears her serious face, a lavender blouse. Sound bites of terror. Another explosion, this one in retaliation for that one. More faces flash across the screen, and it's hard to tell the difference between the terrorists and the terrorized. What I wouldn't give some nights to peek behind the veil, look into the face of God, ask him what it's all about. Mythology? The end times becoming a self-fulfilling prophecy? *There's a hard-hearted rage in people, God. What's that all about?*

The phone rings its old-fashioned ring, and the old minister mutes the television with a click of the remote.

"Yep." He looks at me as if for a cue, but I offer nothing. . . He clears his throat. "Nope. No word from her . . ." He bites his lip, nods. "Is that right?" His voice is a low rasp. "Anybody hurt? . . . Well thank God for that." He shakes his head. . . "Damn fools . . . Yep . . . Sure . . . 'Night."

He sighs as he sets down the receiver. "You got any money, kid?"

"A little. What's up?"

"News ain't good."

I could've told him that much.

"Some fool's been callin' in damn crazy threats, and now they found a pipe bomb rigged under yer car. Cops're takin' this pretty damn serious." He looks up at the ceiling, then back at the TV, switches the thing off.

My lunch feels like dead weight in my belly. I close my eyes, but all I can see are those hands. The sweat. Magdelena's bloodied body in my dream. Seven years closing in on itself. My life. My fellow travelers. *Where are they tonight?* I think of Barbaro's lanky body as he ran down the beach in his pink Speedos. Of Manny, my fat-headed little kitten boy. *A bomb?*

The old minister clears his throat. "Question is, kid, do you have any money?"

"About forty bucks," I tell him. I left my duffel in the car but kept my wallet in the back pocket of my Levi's.

He nods. "You're prob'ly best off stayin' here tonight, but come morning you oughtta head out. Know anybody 'round here?"

I shake my head.

He taps his leg, eyes unfocused. "I might know someone." He stands up with a sigh. "Damned embarrassing time to be a Christian," he mumbles as he shuffles off.

I dream of burning crosses that bleed wine.

The knock on the guest room door in the still-dark morning startles me back to the dense world: "Up and at 'em, kid!"

I dress quickly in the lamplight. Jeans and boots, *Sesame Street* T-shirt over the red camisole. How was I to know when I got dressed in the Super 8 Motel room in Red Bluff that this outfit would soon be all I had? I only wore the T-shirt to please Manny.

I thank the old minister for his help and the hot mug of black coffee he hands me when I walk into the kitchen.

"No bother at all," he says. He's wearing silk pajamas that make me wonder if there ever was a Mrs. Old Minister. He sets down his coffee, unfolds a ragged map of California. "Now," he says, "I've got an old friend up here." He points to a blotch of green to the east. "Know the area?"

I shake my head. I'm always amazed how many areas I still don't know. A girl could travel for a lifetime, and still there'd be vast stretches of landscape and life far off the interstates, unknown.

The old minister leans over the table, draws a squiggling map on a ripped sheet of notebook paper. "You're gonna get the bus right here." He draws an X, then traces a long line out of the city. "It's gonna let you out right here." He draws another X. "Now, you might have to ask around, but if I recalls the place yer lookin' for is right across from this bus stop here. Yer lookin' for Dot." He scratches his head.

I study the dubious Xs and twisting lines. "Is she expecting me?"

The old minister doesn't answer. "You jus' lay low 'til those fools're onto somethin' else. Ya hear me, kid? Lay low."

Chapter 12

LYING LOW

Stepping out into the silky dawn, I feel alone and alive in a far-off, familiar kind of a way. Reminds me of college. Freshman year. Hiking in the dense redwood forest above campus, the morning sun angling through high branches, my grandmother ten months gone and not a single new friend on the horizon. My loneliness seemed daunting then, but now the soft morning air tastes like blackberry honey, my new fear still vague behind me, just a shadow under the streetlamps. Right turn at the corner, a row of weary porch lights. No footsteps.

A car slows at it approaches from behind. I quicken my pace. The old minister's words echo in my head: *Cops're takin' this pretty damn serious.* But it doesn't seem real. I seesaw between panic and faith. *Oh, Martín, make them blind to me.*

I glance back at the approaching car, an old silver Pinto, a "Y" in the license plate, a "729." The kind of details the cops will ask me for later. A hand moves to fling something from the open passenger-side window, and I jump.

"Morning!" a voice calls as the newspaper alights on a manicured lawn.

Relax, Frankka.

At the bus stop there is:

> *A teenage girl arguing with her cell phone in Chinese.*
> *An Arab guy wearing an "I (heart) Jesus" ski cap.*
> *A fast-food-fat white lady with a shopping cart full of snot-*
> *nosed children.*

I'm the only one who climbs onto the Amador Express when it stops.

Three seventy-five for a ticket, but the driver doesn't have change.

The only other passenger on board, a wild-haired woman with a massive grocery bag of something on her lap, rustles through the pockets of her too-big wool cardigan, counting ones and quarters. "I got seventeen bucks," she calls out as the bus door sighs closed behind me.

"Thanks." I grab onto a seatback, trade her for my twenty, pay my fare, and sit down behind her.

"I know you," she says, voice smooth as whiskey.

"I don't think so." I clear my throat, turn to look out the window.

"I *know* you," she insists. "I know you. I know you." She's staring at me, our faces reflected vaguely in the bus window.

"I show you. I know you. I snow you. I'll show you I know you . . ."

I try to concentrate on my breaths, ignore her. Mental cases don't usually make me uneasy, but I'm not sure if this one's random-mental or read-the-paper-mental. *Oh, make them blind to me.*

I watch through our reflections as we roll out of town and into the suburbs, past the 7-Elevens and the Home Depots, facades of commerce.

"I know you," the woman whispers out the window. "I'll show you I know you. I'll snow you . . ."

I close my eyes, massage my face lightly in my hands, look forward to telling Barbaro this strange epic dream I've had, but I don't wake up. My fellow travelers are far away now. I open my eyes on the still same bus headed east out of Sacramento. We pass dusty antique shops, abandoned churches, and fruit stands as the road ribbons through the kind of towns all the kids just want out of. Friendless billboards advertise Mother Lode hotels and Gold Rush casinos over the state line.

I'm relieved when the woman who knows me stands up, hugging her bag and muttering, "I'll show you," and climbs off the bus in the middle of wind-kissed nowhere.

I think of Tony. Was it just a week ago in Portland when he'd sat on a tall stool in the kitchen of the punk house where we were staying, gesturing dramatically and insisting that this country was on the brink of a civil war? The reds versus the blues, the cities versus the rurals, the bigots versus the queers, the religious literalists versus the mystics? The punks had all nodded into their vegan lasagna.

Tony ran his fingers through his short, loose Afro.

"America is becoming a third world country," someone said.

"Good riddance to the superpower," another one chimed in.

And "What kind of world are we living in when the CIA and the *New York Times* suddenly look like the good guys?"

I listened to them all, wary but not worried. I imagined all the hoboes and the families and the traveling performers of the world huddled together around campfires, keeping the light of humanity burning through it all. A utopian apocalypse. I imagined some sudden sense of tolerant community rippling through the small towns of America, the survivalists coming out to share their canned apricots with strangers. I imagined all the yahoos with their trucks and their guns, shooting aimless into the night, but I imagined all of us sheltered in the basement of a punk house, singing.

Civil war or no, I figured I'd always have my troupe.

"End of the line," the driver barks.

Oh, right. I'm alone.

Out on the street, I study the old minister's squiggly map. X marks the spot, but there's just a greasy diner there. I look both ways before crossing the highway. The smell of a deep fryer, the promise of stale coffee with half-and-half. Dot or no, who can resist a roadside diner at sunrise?

I push open the glass door, hesitate before I make my way to the counter. I sit down on a cracked stool, order orange juice and a cream cheese omelet.

"To go?" the waitress asks. I guess she's hoping I'll leave. She's got stringy brown hair and the worst acne I've ever seen on an adult.

"For here," I tell her.

"Coffee?"

"Sure."

"Strange stranger," she hums.

The regulars all laugh at me under their mustaches as they sip their endless coffees from brown mugs. An unfamiliar country song on the radio.

"I'm looking for somebody named Dot," I pipe up when the waitress pushes my giant plate of eggs across the counter. Blank look on her face.

"Dot's place up the road," the guy sitting next to me offers. He smiles, revealing blackened teeth. "Up by the old bus stop." He gestures with his chin.

I eat my eggs in silence. Burned at the edges, undercooked pale yellow ooze in the middle. A greasy roadside diner is always a disappointment. I never learn my lesson. I pay the bill and grab a few paper napkins.

Outside, a ragged traveler stands with his hand outstretched, dirt caked in his life line. "Got any change?" He adjusts his army surplus pack on his back.

I empty my pockets. After the bus ride and breakfast, I've got a twenty and four ones. I think to give him the ones, but a sudden force like a wind nudge from behind me pushes my right hand forward instead of my left.

"You serious?" He looks at the bigheaded twenty like it's foreign currency. "Thanks, lady."

I follow the highway up to the old bus shelter on the hill, graffitied with "Smash the System" and "Jenny + Chris." The only nearby building, a ramshackle old storefront with no sign.

The wooden door's ajar, so I push it open. "Hello?" A dozen round tables with plastic chairs, a stove at the back of the room, a giant pot of soup simmering on the burner, a crucifix on the back wall. "Hello?" No one but the simmering pot. The smell of onions. A handwritten sign on a Formica counter says: "Lunch Served at Noon."

I have to pee. I tiptoe past the stove, knock before opening the door that says Restroom. Opposite the toilet, a Greenpeace poster informs me that it takes ninety years to grow a roll of paper, and suddenly I don't want to wipe. I sit there for a long time, trying to decide what to do before I realize it probably took at least ten years to grow that poster, so I go ahead and take a little toilet paper, Greenpeace having lost the moral high ground.

When I step out of the restroom, a skinny guy with thick glasses is stirring the soup.

"Hey," I venture.

He startles, almost knocking over the pot. "Whoa, I didn't know anyone was in here."

"I'm sorry, I—"

He adjusts his glasses. "Lunch isn't served until noon." He's wearing a red and orange tie-dyed T-shirt.

"I'm looking for Dot."

"Well." He bobs his head up and down like one of Manny's plastic toys. "She doesn't come down here much anymore. Anything I can help you with?"

I shake my head. "Do you know where I can find her?"

He points to the ceiling. "She's up, uh . . ."

I think he's going to say she's dead.

"She's, you know, well, you wanna drive about forty, forty-five miles up the highway, right? Up to Kay's Resort. There's a gas station and a store up there. So you park at Kay's Resort, and you just wanna find the trail and start walking around the lake sort of south and west, right? You're gonna pass some picnic tables and a sandy cove and you just wanna keep going—follow that trail about a mile. That's where you'll find her."

"On the lake?"

"Uh-huh." He turns to stir his soup.

This is ridiculous. I want to call Tony, find out what's going on. Maybe I can get the bus back to Sacramento, meet up with my troupe. Maybe it's not as bad as the old minister made it sound. "Listen," I say, "do you have a phone I can use?"

The guy adjusts his glasses again, reminds me suddenly of a potato bug. "Local call?"

"No."

He scratches his head, squints his eyes. "Well, make it quick, will you?" He points to the black rotary phone on the wall, a relic from another time.

It feels strange to dial in circles. One, wait. Four, wait. One, wait. Five, wait.

Magdelena answers on the first ring, her voice all dread. "Hello?"

I just want talk to Tony.

"Who is this?"

I don't know whether to ask for Tony or to say something to Magdelena. *What do I have to say to her?*

"We don't know where the fuck she is, okay? Tell me who you are or I'm calling the cops."

I hang up.

Back outside, I weigh my options: a highway going up or a highway going down. Dense pine forests or open fields dotted with olive trees. I could keep chasing Dot or wander off. I'm heartened by the fact that no one on the road seems to know who I am, that no one cares what I can or maybe cannot do. It's funny, the way it can feel like everybody knows your name, like everybody wants something from you—a thousand twisted mouths calling your name. Then you just turn, run away, slow your running to a walk, and pretty soon even the memory of those voices begins to fade. There's a whole world far off the interstate that doesn't seem to care where you've come from or why.

I look both ways before crossing to the middle of the highway. No traffic. *Up or down?*

After Rose of Lima decided to join an Augustinian convent, she knelt before her image of Mary and asked for guidance. The virgin said nothing, but when Rose finished praying, she couldn't stand up. She called her brother to help her, but even the buff young guy couldn't move Rose's small body.

"All right, then," Rose said to Mary. "If you don't want me to join the convent, I'll drop the idea." With this, she stood up easily.

Rose prayed for a sign—a new idea, anything. Pretty soon a black and white butterfly started visiting at her window each day. The Third Order Dominican nuns wore white tunics with black cloaks, lived at home rather than in a convent. "Ah," Rose said when she recognized the sign. "Right profession, wrong order." So off she went to join her Dominican butterflies.

"Up or down, Mary?"

I'm expecting a butterfly to appear, fluttering directions, but instead an orange Volkswagen Bug buzzes up the hill toward me. I stick out my thumb.

The bug screeches to a halt. A tiny woman with short gray hair leans out the window. "Didn't anyone ever tell you not to hitchhike?"

"I guess they did."

"Well, get in. You're not going to Tahoe, are you?"

I didn't know this road went to Tahoe. "I'm looking for Kay's Resort."

She nods. "Name's Isabel." She scrambles to clear the books and papers and cassette tapes and bags of trail mix off the passenger seat before I climb in. "I used to hitchhike," she laughs. "Dumb, dumb, dumb."

I don't know what to tell her. I usually have my own car?

We drive up past Bob's You Name It junk shop, past lumberyards and lodges, our climb marked by elevation signs at thousand-foot intervals. Melting snowbanks, thick pine groves, road construction. The Volkswagen spits and moans. There's a boom box in the backseat, an old Utah Phillips CD.

"You're not camping, are you? Without any gear?" I can't tell if she's genuinely concerned or just fill-the-silence wondering.

"Not sure," I admit.

"On the run?" she winks.

"Sort of."

Just above seven thousand feet, we pull into a tiny gas station without any attendants.

"My place is a just few miles further up," Isabel says. "If you hike in from here you oughtta find a campsite. It's not legal, but it'll do."

Now, maybe all Sierra lakes look the same, but I can swear I've seen this one before. Church camp with a visiting priest? I can remember building campfires with twigs and sticks, cooking meat and vegetables wrapped in tinfoil, but the memory is wispy and unfocused. I can't hold onto it. A craggy red volcanic mountain rises from the indigo lake, a stranger among rounded green and snowy peaks. *A campsite?*

In the tackle shop/grocery store, the woman behind the old-fashioned register breathes through a plastic tube connected to a blue tank. *Belabored inhale, belabored exhale.* "Can I help you?"

I feel lightheaded. "Do you have any sleeping bags you lend out or anything?"

She shakes her head no. Thinning white hair.

I wander through aisles of chips and marshmallows, picture postcards of chipmunks and Thunder Mountain, *Wish you were here.* I grab a seventy-five-cent packet of onion soup, just add water.

"I'm looking for Dot," I say as the woman pushes those big buttons on her giant cash register.

She nods. "If you head around the lake about a mile you'll find an old cabin. First one you come to after the lagoon."

Belabored inhale, belabored exhale. "Just an old cabin. Stay close to the lakeshore or you'll miss it."

I have to cut off the sandy trail after just a few hundred yards to stay close to the lakeshore. I shove the onion soup packet into my back pocket as I climb over granite boulders, through stands of ponderosa pines and incense cedars. Patches of dry grass spotted with pennyroyal and brilliant paintbrush flowers. The old cabin is half hidden by red firs, lodgepole pines, western juniper.

A few steps to the porch. *Knock, knock.* "Hello?" No answer, but there's an old hand-carved wooden sign on the red door: "Hospitality." I push it open. "Hello?"

I scan the one-room cabin. A gray Mexican rug covers the floor. Stone walls lined with books. In the center of the room there's a wood-burning strove. In front of it, a hand-made table with gnarled legs. Two narrow cots tucked into two far corners. I step inside. No bathroom, no kitchen, no sink. Just a few jars and buckets lined up against a wall. Beeswax candles and a tiny Joan of Arc statue on a shelf. An old-fashioned spinning wheel behind the door. A small wooden desk piled with papers. A book about Thérèse of Lisieux. A quote tacked to the wall: "Love in action is a harsh and dreadful thing compared with love in dreams. —Dostoyevsky."

Next to the table there's a freestanding cupboard. I creep over and open the slatted door. A jar of pickled eel, a bottle of dandelion wine, a few apples and nectarines, a bag of flour and some salt, two bread rolls, a roll of tinfoil, a jar of instant coffee. I pick up an apple, hard and green. Whoever lives here hasn't gone far. I sit down on a wooden stool to wait.

I'm thinking of the little girl with her stained yellow T-shirt who found her way into the locked church in Sacramento. Her hopeful face, her sick father. My remorse tastes like stale bread. I want to rewind to that moment. What could I have done? Surely something. How far had she come to be whisked away without so much as a nod of condolence? I want to rewind further still, to Clatsop Beach with its salt-water breeze, the iridescent sand, Judy's prying questions. That old shipwreck. "Nobody die," the hotel man had told me. "Everybody save. You like."

I climb down the porch steps and make my way along a sandy trail to the lakefront, scan the landscape for any sign of humanity before I strip down to my underwear.

The water feels like an ice floe as I wade in. The trout and guppies can stand it, why not me? Rocks slippery under my feet, a mosquito eater glides on the lake's glassy surface. The giant glistening basin of cool is a blue world without any trouble or shit, egos or money counting, performances or freeway miles.

Dive in.

All quiet and cold.

When I finally emerge from the lake shivering wet, the June sun is sinking over the granite ridge behind the cabin, a reflection of the sunset turning the face of the volcanic mountain shades of amber, red, and purple. Pine needles and pebbles prick at my soles as I carry my clothes back to the cabin porch. Mosquitoes swarm my goose-bumped skin, their bloodsucking buzz-whine some fresh hell. I hurry inside, close the windows and the heavy wooden door, but it's no use. The place is already abuzz. I light a candle, hoping they'll be attracted to a fiery death as I pour myself a cup of watered wine. I wonder when the cabin's rightful sleeper will show. *If she'll show.* Making myself at home in a stranger's house.

I want my saint book, but I guess the napkin I pocketed at the diner this morning will have to do.

Anthony of Egypt
(IF YOU NEED TO CLEAR YOUR HEAD)

A.K.A. Anthony the Abbot, Anthony the Great
FEAST DAY: January 17
SYMBOLS: a pig, a bell, a T-shaped staff

Hasn't everyone heard the Gospel story of the rich young man who comes to Jesus saying, "I've followed all your commandments. What more can I do?"

"Go and sell all you have," Jesus tells him. "Give it to the poor, and you will have treasures in heaven."

We hear it, do nothing, but when Anthony of Egypt heard the tale back in the third century, some rusty engine inside of him turned over. The barely literate orphan son of prosperous merchants sold most of what his parents had left him, gave the money to the poor.

Back at church, he again heard the Gospel. "Be not solici-
tous of tomorrow."

He gave away the rest of his belongings, made his way out
into the Libyan desert to take up residence in an abandoned
tomb. He spent his days in prayer, ate only after sunset—a little bread and water. He slept on the bare ground, welcoming
angels and battling old psychic demons. Even without possessions or contact with friends, it took Anthony thirteen years to
clear his mind.

He crossed out of the desert then.

On the other side of the Nile, he found an old fort on a
mountain and lived there for another twenty years, tending a
little garden of food and herbs. Pilgrims came knocking, but
Anthony refused to see them, preferring his solitude. Gradually,
a number of would-be disciples established themselves in
caves and huts around the mountain—a colony of ascetics.
They begged Anthony to come out and preach what he knew, to
guide them on the spiritual path. When he finally yielded and
emerged from his self-imposed poverty and solitude, he wowed
them all with his glowing health and soul's joy.

"How'd you get so foxy?" they wanted to know.

Middle-aged by now, but Anthony looked like some strap-
ping Adonis. "Well," he explained. "Let me tell you what I've been
doing these last thirty-three years . . ."

Up until then, it had been cool for Christians to live simply,
abstain from marriage, starve themselves, pray and work in
service to the poor—but they'd done it all without leaving
home. Anthony preached total withdrawal from the rat race,
attracted crowds of pagan and Christian followers. He
founded a monastery of scattered cells—didn't want anything

to do with stately buildings and well-laden tables. When that community seemed to be running well, he headed east toward the Red Sea. In a desolate place near a spring of fresh water, he established a new hermitage. Passing caravans and shepherds left gifts of dates, bread, and onions. Ten thousand monks and twice that many nuns followed him, and his example sparked a sweeping monastic movement.

Anthony was 105 years old when he finally gave away his hair shirt, his old cloak, and the two sheepskins he'd slept on, saying, "Farewell, ye that are my heartstrings, for Anthony is going and will not be with you in this world anymore."

When you need to clear your head, just pray to that old hermit Anthony. He'll soothe your depression, your inertia, your claustrophobia, and your funky skin conditions. His feast is celebrated in mid-January when cool Saturn rules the sky. After all the ruckus of the holidays, Anthony reminds us that the cure for both alienation and loneliness is solitude.

If you've abdicated your right to create your own life story, vow to take it back. If you're ruled by your possessions, give them away. By a toxic lover, diplomatically take your leave. By addictions, wean yourself with compassion, and if that doesn't work, go find a quiet shelter on a mountaintop, far from liquor stores and dealers. Welcome angels as you breathe through your parade of demons.

When you've finally cleared your head—after thirteen hours or thirteen years—descend from the mountain and do your work in the world.

The only sound now, the crickets. Or are they cicadas? The evening is a chill. Blanket of stars. Darkening moonless night.

Inside the cabin, I fumble around by candlelight, find a single pan on the bottom shelf of the freestanding cupboard, help myself to a multigrain roll.

I take a few small logs from the woodpile on the porch, gather sticks in the dark behind the cabin. I should have prepared the fire before sunset.

In a blackened round of granite stones between the cabin and the shore, I arrange the firewood, waste a whole book of matches trying to light the thing. *I hope Magdelena falls from her trapeze and Lupe doesn't catch her. Splat.*

Finally some promising embers. I blow just hard enough to redden them. Sweet blue-orange flames. Life must have been a bitch before matches.

The water takes forever to boil, tiny bubbles gathering at the bottom of the pan like a reluctant audience. I mix enough soup for two. Maybe my invisible host will show up. Maybe I'll save it for tomorrow.

The salty hot from my Sierra cup burns my tongue, soothes my throat. I chase it with watered dandelion wine. I count shooting stars, breathe the cool mountain air. Silence is part of the sound here, and if you listen long enough, the past becomes an echo and the future just a likely story. *I could leave the world of people and hurt forever.*

Chapter 13

AFTER-SCHOOL CAKE

I must have been about eleven years old the afternoon I walked home from school under thick gray clouds, said good-bye to Saint Dympna at the door, climbed the dirty red stairs to our apartment, and found it empty.

"Nana?"

I was old enough to be left alone, but I panicked. "Nana?" She'd never not been there, dusting plastic fruit or crying depressed in her armchair, muttering her rosary or waiting at the kitchen table with a glass of apple juice and a triangle of bready cake. "Nana?"

I rushed into her room: empty. The bathroom, empty too. Then down the back stairs to Peggy's apartment.

She looked up from the Tarot cards spread out on her kitchen table like a meal. "Sorry, Frances. I haven't seen her all day."

Across the street to Kim's Groceries: "No. She no come today."

Nana had no friends, few appointments.

I ran the seven blocks to the old stone church in the early winter drizzle. *Maybe she suddenly came up with some ancient sin she had to confess?* But Father Michaels's office was abandoned.

"Where is she?" I begged the dim-lit image of Our Lord above the altar. All the times I'd wished her dead, gone, or disappeared rushed to mind like a mudslide. All the times she wouldn't let me go to the Esprit Outlet or Stonestown Mall on the bus; all the times I knew I couldn't bring anyone home to play jacks in the green-carpeted living room because she'd be there in her stupid old chair, weeping like a stupid old woman. *I swear I didn't mean it.*

I walked home slowly under the magnolias, the sounds of the city fading into a faraway clamor. I climbed the red-carpeted stairs, pushed open the door to our still-empty apartment, sat down at the blue kitchen table to wait. Maybe she got lost somewhere. Maybe she took the wrong bus and ended up in Hunter's Point. What if she was hit by a car? What if she wasn't carrying any identification? The last dusky light of day sighed through the windowpane. The white-faced clock on the kitchen wall ticked away the seconds and minutes and hours. I waited like a four-year-old for her parents. *Sometimes people just never come home.* Finally. Eight o'clock. A fumbling at the door. "Nana?" Tears welled up in my eyes.

She wobbled in, smelling of beer and the faint residue of a smoky room. "I'm so late," she giggled.

I stared at her. "Where were you, Nana?"

"Oh," she blushed. "Didn't you start dinner?"

"Where were you?"

But my Nana just sighed. "Oh, child, there were decades when I never worried about anyone's after-school cake." She lumbered into her room and closed the white door behind her.

Neither of us ate.

Decades?

Chapter 14
DOT

"Good morning, Goldilocks."

I open my eyes in the pillowy impressionist light of the cabin. Exposed wood beams on the ceiling. I start to sit up, disoriented. The far drumming of a woodpecker reminds me of where I am, how I got here. "I'm sorry, I—"

The voice stands at the table, stirring instant coffee crystals into steaming mugs. She's old, but I can't tell how old, white hair braided into a coronet around her head. Tall and slightly disheveled, she wears a shapeless blue housedress.

"The old minister in Sacramento sent me, I—" I climb out of bed, still dressed in my dusty jeans and *Sesame Street* T-shirt.

"I like a girl who sleeps in her clothes," the voice winks. "You never know when they'll come for you."

I run my fingers through my hair, nervous as a thief.

Outside the open window, a hawk glides from its perch.

"I waited up," I start to explain.

"Was I out past my curfew?" She smiles, pushes a mugful of black coffee across the table in my direction. Austere features, strong jaw, not a stitch of makeup on her face. "I'd lock the door if I wanted to keep the riffraff out."

"I guess you would." I sip the unsweetened coffee.

"Dot," she says as she offers me a hunk of dark rye bread, places another next to her own mug on the table. "Dorothy, really." She moves for the door, the heel of the loaf in hand. "Breakfast!" she calls from the porch. A long, low whistle.

I watch through the doorway as the jays and orange-breasted robins glide down from the pines. A few chipmunks scurry up the stairs.

"Don't mind our guest," Dorothy whispers. "She's just passing through."

The creatures sing and cluck, all sounding at once.

Dorothy laughs as she distributes the rye crumbs. "Well, maybe she's a city girl."

A pang of self-consciousness—*Are they talking about me?*—then embarrassment folding in on itself as it occurs to me that I'm actually worrying what a bunch of birds and rodents might think of me.

Relax, Frankka.

"Does beauty make you uncomfortable?" Dorothy wants to know when I tiptoe out to join her on the porch.

"No," I say sheepishly.

"That's good. All this life force blossoming makes some people a little bit nervous. First shoots of green pushing up through the earth, and people start picking fights, dropping bombs." She rinses her coffee mug in a blue bucket, stares out over the still pewter lake. "Cynicism," she hums.

The golden light on the far forested shore fills me with a sudden dread. Maybe beauty does make me a little bit uncomfortable.

"Are you planning to introduce yourself?" Dorothy asks.

I hadn't planned either way. I take a deep breath. The chilled morning air. "Frankka," I offer.

"And what brings you to the mountains without a pack, Frankka?"

A giant ant inches across a red-brown porch board, carrying the lifeless body of another. I'm pleased with myself for finding this hideaway, hostess and all, but I'm anxious, too. There's something disarming about my host. *What brings me to the mountains without a pack?* I'm surprised when I hear myself answer her, "My friends turned out to be a bunch of backstabbing bitches."

Dorothy laughs. "A common problem. You're fleeing that?"

I guess I am. Fleeing that. I think to tell Dorothy about the rest of it—my road weariness and insomnia; the clip-clop of the reporter's boots as she strode into the Pig 'N Pancake, sniffing after tragedy; the church crowd spilling out into blistering Sacramento streets, the air around them thick with some desperate kind of faith; the old minister's warning, *Cops're takin' this pretty damn serious;* the highway up from the bus shelter, green with the promise of cover—but I say nothing.

Dorothy wraps cheese and fruit in napkins, places the bundles in a black tote bag. "I'm going for a hike," she says. "Come along?"

I'm half-sure Dorothy represents some waking dream, my intrinsic loneliness manifesting a caretaker, but I pull on my boots.

The morning sun is just a bright pledge from the other side of the mountains as we climb through sagebrush and manzanita shrub, up angled masses of gray granite cut by ancient glaciers. Black flecks glimmer like mysterious jewels in the gray-white rock. Tiny succulents and clusters of pink flowers that look like kittens' paws push upward through the sandy dirt. We grab hold of ledges to steady our climb, rest on natural stone benches. Trees spring improbably from the soft turf between ridges, their red branches gnarled by alpine winds. We hike in silence.

Even in her housedress and comfortable shoes, Dorothy effortlessly catches her stride.

I scramble to keep up with her as she eases down a shadowed cliff. It's not lost on me, the fact that I'm following a total stranger off trail into the Sierra outback like some creepy scene from *Unsolved Mysteries,* but there's a cool wind on my shoulders, and even as I'm tripping to keep pace with Dorothy, some blind confidence whispers I'm where I need to be.

In the swampy flat of an emerald glen at the foot of a granite amphitheater, Dorothy sits on a fallen log, sets her old tote bag down next to her. Big-leafed hellebores and tiny white violets carpet the moist earth. "So what's this about your friends?"

Where to begin? "I had a troupe," I tell her.

"A theater troupe?" Her eyes bright.

"Yeah." The smell of fresh mud, spring turning to summer. "A theater troupe" doesn't quite sum it up, though, does it? *Famiglia* was more like it. How to explain? My little gang of kindred who seemed to get the joke of life, of the world. They saw everything for the messed-up, over-hyped show it is. A shared displacement. They cared about the constantly twisting interpretation of all the old stories. They could feel the shocking beauty of a freight train, steady as a heartbeat. They believed in fate and flight. They understood the tedious nightmare it is when you get cornered in a bar with someone wanting to know if you're Saved—some drunk who wants you to go to heaven with him.

"And now?" Dorothy asks.

I stare at the greening earth. "I don't know," I admit. "I had a troupe and now I don't."

Dorothy leans forward to stretch her back.

I want to be a glacier, but even when I will myself hard and solid, I only seem to manage a brittle facade—a lacquer-thin sheet of ice on the lake's surface. I say, "There's a meanness in people, you know? A greed. I used to think it was just *out there* in the world, but now I see that it's in everyone. There's a violence. When I was a kid, they taught me about evil and sin and all that—about meanness—but they taught me it could be exorcised, driven out. I believed that. But it turns out people are really shitty. You're left with this impossible choice: You can trust no one, tell your stories to no one, become a hermit or a lone traveler or something. Or you can just expect betrayal. You can swallow hard and expect betrayal. The worst part is that it's in me, too—the meanness. I get to hear my own justifications whispered under my breath, but that doesn't change anything." I must sound like some babbling adolescent.

"Listen," Dorothy says.

No sound.

Shhh.

A quick rustling behind me. *What is it?*

Dorothy fumbles around in her bag, produces a smooth, fat nectarine. "Just life," she says, then bites into the orange fruitflesh. Juice dribbles down her chin and onto her neck. It occurs to me that Dorothy must have been a beauty in her day. It's not so much that she's lost her looks, either. It's just that it takes a while to notice because you never see a face like hers on television.

"Where you from, anyway?"

"A lot of places," Dorothy says. "Oakland. Chicago. New York." She sets a crumble of cheese on the log next to her. "Go ahead."

A walnut-colored chipmunk with two white stripes down its back darts up onto the log, gives me a sideways glance before taking off with the cheese.

I want to ask Dorothy how old she is but decide the question might be rude. "Lived here long?" I try.

She sort of nods and shakes her head at the same time. "I lived in New York City."

I can't picture Dorothy in New York City. Strange that a person can live somewhere long enough to claim it and still not have a hint of the place on their skin.

"Wait," Dorothy says. She leaves her bag on the log as she steals off between some trees. *Did she hear something?*

I'm alone in the glen for what feels like a long time, building New York City lives for Dorothy in my imagination. She's an East Village beatnik bohemian in the late fifties. She's a Harlem armed revolutionary in the late sixties. She's a Broadway star, maybe, belting out campy show tunes with Carol Channing.

"Sending your mind on wild goose chases?" Dorothy asks as she hands me a Sierra cup of icy stream water.

"No," I lie.

"I was a journalist," she says flatly, then takes a long drink. Just what I need. Another journalist.

"So you sat around waiting for tragedy?"

Dorothy wrinkles her nose. "Hardly. You never accomplish anything with fear and horror stories."

Thérèse of Lisieux

(IF YOU NEED A LITTLE LOVE)

A.K.A. The Little Flower, The Saint of the Little Way
FEAST DAY: October 1
SYMBOLS: violets, roses, wildflowers

The Lord set the book of nature before Thérèse of Lisieux, and she saw that all the flowers he had created were lovely. The splendor of the rose and the whiteness of the lily didn't rob the little violet of its scent or the daisy of its simple charm. Thérèse realized that if every tiny flower wanted to be a rose, spring would lose its loveliness and there would be no wildflowers to make the meadows sing. *It's just the same in the world of souls,* she thought. God had created great saints like lilies and roses, but also much lesser saints who had to be content to live as the daisies or the violets that rejoiced his eyes whenever he glanced down. *Perfection means doing God's will*—that's what Thérèse figured. *I will be that which God wants me to be.*

Read about Thérèse in sourcebooks or encyclopedias and her story might sound like pious drivel, but look at the photographs of the moon-faced nun, look into her eyes, imagine the determined little girl from Normandy who wanted only to please God.

In 1877, when Thérèse was four years old, her mother died of cancer, and her father moved the family to Lisieux. Both parents had dreamed of cloistered lives for themselves, encouraged their children's religious interests, but Thérèse seemed downright obsessed. A sickly kid, she was temporarily cured when a statue of the Blessed Virgin smiled at her.

"Oh, when can I join the convent?" she cried.

"Come back when you're grown," a solemn-faced mother superior told her, shaking her head.

Her father thought she should wait, too. She was only a kid, after all, and one often delirious with fever.

She appealed to an uncle, then to the bishop.

Not only did Thérèse want to be a nun, she intended to be a saint. And she had a strategy. She called her path the Little Way of love in action—total trust in God. She'd train herself to respond to every chore, every encounter, and every insult with love. Birds gathered at her feet to hear her strategy. "I'm the Little Flower," she said. A hippie chick before her time. She had no grand plans—just the radical belief that she could fulfill her destiny simply by being herself.

At age fifteen, Thérèse traveled to Rome with her father, begged the pope himself for permission to join a convent.

Ol' Leo XIII told the girl it would happen if God willed it.

Well, God must have willed it, because Thérèse went home and took the veil as a Carmelite nun.

She moved into her new cell, but at first she felt like she'd lost her calling. *What am I doing here?* God was silent.

Pretty soon, teenage mood swings sent Thérèse careening back and forth between ecstatic joy and bitter sadness. *Love,* she told herself. *Stick to the Little Way.* But convent life didn't provide easy peace. One sister had an annoying way of fidgeting with her rosary. Another splashed Thérèse with dirty water at the laundry sink. Therese thought, *I must pray for her even though her attitude makes me believe she has no love for me.* How can a girl learn forgiveness, after all, if she's got no one to forgive? *I will be love,* Thérèse vowed.

She persisted through all the aggravations of community life and through the illness—always the illness—recurring, painful, draining.

After seven years in the convent, maybe it all got to be too much for her. Maybe she missed her mother. Maybe she couldn't imagine waiting another moment to see the face of God. She closed her eyes, wanted to give up. She offered herself in prayer as a victim to divine merciful love. She'd begun reciting the stations of the cross, preparing for death, when—cometlike—a fiery flash darted from the magic vault of heaven and pierced through her chest and into her four-chambered heart. She thought she'd die right there from the rush of pain and love: unconditional, unconditional.

Her sister Pauline, now the prioress at the convent, could see that Thérèse wasn't long for this world. She instructed her to begin writing a spiritual memoir.

Bird friends sang at the window as Thérèse wrote. She continued her daily chores through her fatigue, but by year's end it was obvious to everyone: tuberculosis. Thérèse's superiors relieved her of her duties. She should spend all of her energy writing *The Story of a Soul*.

When she finished her pages, Thérèse set down her pen and, surrounded by birds, the Little Flower died, crying, "My God! I love thee!"

She would spend her heaven doing good on earth.

Dead at the age of twenty-four, Thérèse had founded nothing, built no great pyramids or shrines. Just a motherless and sickly kid, she learned to live in her community and imagined, largehearted, that we were all saints-in-progress.

"Our Lord does not look so much at the greatness of our actions, nor even at their difficulty, but at the love with which we do them."

Even Jesus died a failure.

She said, "For me, prayer is a surge of the heart; a simple look turned toward heaven; a cry of recognition and of love, embracing both trial and joy."

Patron saint of air crews, florists, AIDS sufferers, and orphans, those who know her pray to Thérèse. Broke and desperate, sick and suffering, blocked and annoyed, they pray. In their dreams, she brings them money, fresh determination, the energy to forgive. Come morning, her gifts sparkle real as granite.

Honor Thérèse by walking the Little Way of love in action. Say, "God, help me to simplify my life by learning what you want me to be and becoming that person." Build an altar with gold paper hearts and flowers—violets if you can find them. Say, "Thérèse, you were little, but bad-ass. Teach me to be such an awesome failure."

"Are you Catholic?" I ask Dorothy as we're gathering wood for the fire at dusk. I'm thinking of the Saint Thérèse book and the Joan of Arc statue in her cabin.

"Oh, yes," Dorothy says, looking up.

Her affirmation sounds strange. Not "was" or "lapsed" or "recovering." No apologies. Just "Oh, yes."

"Why do you ask?" she smiles, her stern features casting quick shadows across her face.

"I just—you know—the church is such bullshit. All the rules and the hierarchy."

Dorothy arranges twigs and cut logs in the circle of blackened stones, ignites the thing with a single match, sets a pot of water to boil. "We're all Christ and we all get crucified. What's hierarchical about that?"

I guess I never thought of it that way.

Dorothy stares across the lake into the darkening blue. "You can worry about the hierarchy of the church if you like—someone has to—but more importantly, there comes a time when you have to start making a choice, don't you think?"

"A choice?"

"Yes. A daily choice. You can wake up each morning thinking about all the backstabbers in this world, about all the people who have betrayed you, about everything that has been taken from you. Or you can open your eyes and you can ask yourself, 'What's my love strategy today?'" Dorothy bends pasta into the boiling water, stirs it as it softens. She arranges cubes of pickled eel on tin plates, grabs the handles of the pot with her bare hands, and removes it from the fire. In an iron skillet, she crushes a garlic clove, pours in a little oil. She fries the garlic with a handful of peppers and herbs, adds the cooked pasta. "It's not much," she says, heaping it onto the plates next to the eel, "but it'll do." She empties what's left of the dandelion wine into our Sierra cups. "Anyway," she says. "Everyone has to have a strategy, don't you think?"

I shrug. I'm more impressed with her quick dinner.

"The question is," she points her fork in my direction, "is it a war strategy or a love strategy?"

I take a bite of pasta, sip my wine. "Of course you have to have a war strategy if you're going to war. In war you have to take things over, fight. You have to win. But love. I mean, love just happens."

She nods, wipes her mouth with her hand. In the light of the campfire, her face looks like something otherworldly. "Is that your experience?" she asks. "That love just happens?"

Delicious as her herbed pasta and eel dinner is, Dorothy is starting to bug me. Weird frumpy woodswoman who talks to birds.

"I wouldn't mind living out here like you do," I say, changing the subject. "But not so close to the trail. I'd build my cabin way up there." I point to a far snowcapped mountain on the other side of the lake. A star shoots across the night sky, but there are so many of them, you'd hardly miss it. I think I can hear children singing campfire songs on a far shore.

Dorothy shakes her head. "Oh, Frankka. Anyone can be a saint on a mountaintop."

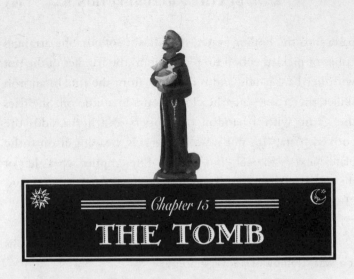

Chapter 15
THE TOMB

Once, just once, my grandmother took me on a Muni bus to the giant concrete passport office in San Francisco.

I couldn't stand still in line. I tapped my sneaker incessantly on the cold floor. "Where are we going?"

"A holy place" is all Nana would tell me.

On the airplane, my ears ached. I ate the saltiest macaroni I'd ever tasted, threw up in the white waxed paper bag.

As we made our way through a long line of travelers at the foreign airport, my grandmother complained that her ankles had swollen like watermelons. An airport worker offered her a wheelchair, and I pushed her to the immigration booth, where she spoke to the uniformed official in a language I didn't understand. Red stamps in our new passports.

An endless bus ride, we sweat like elephants. Everything smelled of garlic as we passed cornfields and vineyards, vast golden landscapes dotted with cypresses, olive trees, and giant round hay bales.

At a rest stop, a German tourist bought me a hollow chocolate egg with a toy turtle in it.

At the red plastic table outside, stray chickens pecked at our shoes.

"Bella Umbria," my grandmother sighed.

We piled back onto the bus, barreled farther through the foreignness until, at last, a castle of a city rose up from the countryside, the color of old bone.

My classmates at All Saints K–8 had written compositions about summer vacations they'd taken with their families, so I'd imagined a grand hotel or cozy log cabin. Instead, we hiked uphill to a dusty pilgrim's hostel run by nuns who wore scratchy brown habits, and we shared a room with a half dozen old people who muttered in Italian even as they slept.

When Nana went to bed and I lingered in the arched doorway, the sisters invited me to play cards with them in a damp brick room. Five-card stud and I won 3,000 lire! The nuns chuckled, slapped their knees. I quit while I was ahead, climbed into the cot next to my grandmother's, and slept the sleep of a rich girl, dreaming of turquoise swimming pools and shrimp cocktails from Fisherman's Wharf. Imagine my disappointment in the morning when all that 3,000 lire bought was a tin bracelet in a souvenir shop. Still, I kept that bracelet and my little plastic turtle for years.

Morning in Assisi, and we made our way through the touristed streets to a courtyard in front of the rose-windowed basilica. "Before Francis, this was the Hill of Hell," a near tour guide explained. "He chose to be buried at the very place where public executions were once held."

Inside, I craned my neck to the high ceilings, frescoed like the night sky—gold stars on indigo. *A holy place.* I studied the images on the walls depicting my namesake's life from madness to ecstasy. The supernatural radiance of God's love. "Pray," my grandmother instructed me. "Ask forgiveness."

I followed her down a wide staircase and through a gothic portal. A second church lived in half-light. "Look," my grandmother pointed. A fresco of the Madonna with angels, and Saint Francis showing off his stigmata.

We descended lower still. Pale and dim. Just a few brass lamps burned like stars in the chilled basement. "Come," my grandmother whispered. She knelt silently at the crypt. This is what we'd come so far to behold—the porous bricks over Saint Francis's body, deep underground.

"Come and touch, my child."

The tomb.

Imagined earthquakes rattled in my mind. *What if we got trapped down here?* The saint's decomposing body. *Touch it?*

A young monk sang softly from the corner. In his thick brown cape, he reminded me of an Ewok from *Star Wars.*

I didn't want to touch it.

Nana's hand trembled on the stone wall of the tomb. "Come and be forever blessed, child."

She took my hand, pulled me toward the dark shrine.

I lowered my body as if kneeling, but I didn't let my knees touch the stone steps.

"There, my child," Nana whispered.

I reached forward as she had, pretending to touch the outer wall of the tomb, but I let my dirty fingers hover there in nothingness above the dark stones.

My grandmother whispered, "Yes. You are cleansed."

I pulled back, stood up too quickly, stepped to the right so another pilgrim could be forever blessed.

As we ascended the stairs, Nana held my hand tightly, her fingernails digging into my scarred and unblessed palm.

That night, after she'd fallen asleep and I played one-eyed jacks with the sisters and won nothing, I lay awake on my cot, replaying the visit to that candlelit basilica basement in my mind. Everything might have been different if I'd only touched the tomb. *Why couldn't I touch it?* Later, my grandmother would brag about our pilgrimage. If I got a B+ in algebra or played my scales flawlessly on the piano, she'd tell my teachers, "She touched the tomb of Saint Francis, you know?" As if this explained my every minor success.

If only.

I felt hotly jealous of Assisi—*who's jealous of a place?*—but that town soothed my grandmother like a lover, brought a lightness to her face no childish accomplishment or sudden bleeding ever could. The cloak of life-is-sorrow she wore like a favorite sweater seemed mystically to lift. She smiled, her dark eyes bright. Even with all the walking, she didn't complain about her edema or her joints.

Back home, the depression returned. Of course it returned. But for that one precious week, my grandmother floated. She'd touched the tomb of Saint Francis, you know?

Chapter 16

HANDS

The morning is a glare. Every muscle in my body aches.

Dorothy stands, a silhouette in the doorway, her black tote bag slung over her shoulder. "I'm expecting quite a few people tonight," she says. "You'll have to take the canoe over to the store and get some wine. Then see what you can do about dinner. I'll be back by seven." She turns.

I rub my eyes. "Huh?" I gather my bones to stand, confusion morphing into annoyance. "Dorothy!"

But she's already gone.

I have $3.60 in my pocket, no idea how to steer a canoe. *What kind of hospitality is this?*

A hot mug of black coffee waits for me on the table, but no further instructions. I sit dumbly sipping the coffee. *Wine? Dinner?*

I could leave this place, probably should, but where would I go? Hike back out to the road, hitch a ride somewhere? Maybe up to Tahoe. I could cross the state line, play my $3.60 in the slots, win big. Maybe catch a Greyhound east. Denver. Surely no one reads the *L.A. Times* in Denver. I could get a job as a waitress in some roadside diner. Instant coffee dreams. *What have I gotten myself into?*

Outside, the yellow-painted wooden canoe lies upside down, a giant banana on the lakeshore. It takes most of my strength to turn the thing over, slide it into the water.

I find two oars propped against a pine tree, grab one of them, but when I turn around the boat is already floating away. *Shit.*

I pull my boots off, wade into the freezing lake, manage to catch the thing and climb aboard without tipping it over. I sit on the cloth-covered seat at the helm, start paddling, but the boat just turns like the hand of a clock. I try rowing on the other side. Full counterclockwise rotation.

A bald guy sitting out on his tin boat in the lake laughs at me, sips his morning beer. "You gotta steer that thing from the back!"

"What?"

"Turn your ass around!"

Right.

But even from the back, the long narrow boat is no cinch to maneuver. Left sends me right and right send me left. I have to keep switching sides, battling a south wind intent on blowing me off course. The water that splashes onto my hands and arms is icy, as if this gorgeous clear lake is the very source of all cold. If I capsized, could I swim to safety? I wobble in the general direction of Kay's Resort, a reddish wood dollhouse on the far shore. *I should have walked.*

A few kids kick around in a beachy lagoon, but otherwise the lake is quiet.

As the water shallows, I jump out of the boat, frightening a few Canadian geese and soaking my jeans. I drag the thing the rest of the way to the shore.

The grocery store/tackle shop's aisles are stacked with canned wieners and Screaming Yellow Zonkers, marshmallows and packets of beef jerky.

A sunburned man wearing suspenders buys beer and bait. "Where's the best place to catch trout?" he asks the woman behind the register.

"In the water," she grumbles.

The orange price sticker on the gallon of Gallo: $8.88.

I wait for the man to leave, hoping the woman behind the register will be more generous without a witness. I show her my money. "Can I pay you the other five-something later?" I'm trying to sound as young and earnest as possible—at once worthy of pity and trust.

"Mmm-mmm," she shakes her head. *Belabored inhale, belabored exhale.*

I guess I'm not a kid anymore.

I start to hoist the glass jug back up on the shelf when she says, "I got some garbage out back you can take down to the pit for me."

"Oh, sure."

She directs me through a storeroom piled with boxes, past a walk-in fridge.

I'm thinking there's a big bag of garbage out there, maybe two, but when I open the back door a veritable dump rots in the cool glare. Piles of crushed beer cans, giant black plastic bags lined up like bodies. *Unbelievable.*

"Where's the pit?" I ask a gray-haired guy in overalls who stands chopping wood at a stump.

He chuckles to himself, like maybe I'm not the first fool who's fallen for the "got some garbage" line.

"Up thataway about a quarter mile." He points in the opposite direction from Dorothy's cabin.

Great.

I think of Thérèse of Lisieux—*I will be love*—but I'm not feeling it. *I will be sucker* is more like it. I carry the stinking bags of god-knows-what two at a time up a narrow grassy trail marked by stacked stones, cursing all the way, the incessant tweeting of some damned bird following me like a starstruck stalker.

It's got to be noon when I finally stumble back into the little store, fresh with the stench of a thousand city-campers' refuse. "It's all in the pit," I announce bitterly.

"Then the wine's all yours," the woman says. "Take two if you like."

I carry the jugs out to my yellow boat, place them in the center before I push it into the water and climb back in. Four strokes on the left, four strokes on the right. I'm paddling rhythmically, some kind of rowing meditation, when a sudden western wind picks up, making whitecap waves of the lake's surface and pushing me toward the wrong shore. I paddle furiously on the left, hoping to go right, but the boat turns itself around. *Oh, come on.*

I row on this side, now the other. "Home," I whisper, paddling wildly through the waves, but I'm just careening willy-nilly toward an island. A scraping sound. *Bash, jolt.* A creak, snap. The sharp jut of a half-submerged granite boulder pokes up through the wooden bottom of my yellow canoe. Without thinking, I jump out into the freezing water, start kicking like mad, pushing the boat toward the closest land. My legs feel like rubber. I close my eyes, push onward. *Go, go.* Laughter echoes in my head. I look up and around—*who's laughing at me?*—but there's no one. Just a vast rippling lake in the wind, green, granite and red-brown volcanic mountains rising up around me. Quick breath of air, I try to pull myself back aboard the half-sunk boat, but the thing rolls. *The wine!*

I'm just a few strokes from shallow water, splashing like a caught seal, cold drenched pathetic as I finally pull the canoe onto the shore of a sandy rock island.

Just inland between two firs, I can see a clearing, a bright yellow tent. I'm an intruder on someone's private summer getaway with a busted boat and no wine.

I leave my boat, follow the shore to the east, skirting the campsite, surveying where I've landed. On the far side of the small island, I harvest a few handfuls of pine nuts from the dense branches of a tree, pull two sprigs of what smells like thyme, walk on.

I climb a rounded gray rock in full sunlight, lay my clothes to dry next to me, and stretch out, willing the sun to dissolve me into steam. A quick prayer to Saint Thérèse: "Send me some counsel, Little Flower, will you? I'm seven thousand feet up. I could climb higher, or I could head back down."

But Thérèse is silent.

"Don't you remember me?" I beg.

An insect buzzes in my ear, and I start thinking about all the ways in which Dorothy really is a loser: that shapeless housedress, those nun shoes, no boyfriend, probably no kids, no running water. Her outhouse smells like shit. I bet she couldn't even make it as a journalist. Why else would she be out here in nowhereland? Probably doesn't have a friend in the world. Expecting quite a few people for dinner? *Yeah, right.* Where does she think they're gonna come from? The bottom of the lake? Quite a few people, huh? Batty old woman with her braided coronet.

I guess I closed my eyes because just then a stark dream juts into the afternoon. Two severed hands on a granite rock at the side of a grassy trail. I stop to check them out. They're a woman's hands, surely, with short, rounded nails. A silver ring on the right thumb. I guess they've been here a long time because they're not bleeding at the severed place. But they're pink, as if still alive. I crouch closer. They smell like violets. I pick one up, turn it over. A dark pink scar in the middle of the palm, a deep life line, a faint love line. I grab the other one. *My hands.*

I sit up too fast, shield my eyes from the sun. I check my hands to make sure they're still attached.

The voice of a little boy floats up from somewhere below. He's singing "Oh, Susanna" at the top of his lungs.

Chapter 17

WHY GOD HAS SO FEW FRIENDS

I was seventeen years old when it finally dawned on me that God really had to be an asshole.

Nana had seemed tired the night before, so I let her sleep in. I left a fresh butter croissant on her bedside table, called Peggy downstairs, and asked her to come up and check on her midmorning. It wasn't a big deal. Nana hadn't been well since she'd fallen and broken her hip when I was in ninth grade. After two weeks at San Francisco General, she was a shell of the woman I'd called Nana. Never regained the little strength she'd had, walked only as if leaving.

Each week she could do less, and each week she imagined that more had to be done. "Did you sterilize the apples before you sliced them?"

"Yes, Nana," I said, swishing the red fruit under a jet of cold water. I took on the housework, the laundry, and the cooking, tried to let Nana alone with her quiet rosary prayers and her rest. We exchanged her old twin frame and mattress for a hospital bed she could adjust up and down. She watched Peter Jennings on TV.

That morning, it took everything I had not to doze off in calculus. Social studies was all crusades and conquests, democracy versus empire, murder for money dressed up as murder for God. Someone slipped me a note: *U R not gonna believe who Annie made out with at Aaron's party. Take a hall pass and meet me in the bathroom.* But as soon as I stepped into the hallway with my wooden pass, here comes plain-clothed Sister Roberta click-clogging down the hall in her big black shoes.

"Frances Catherine!" She said it like it was the answer to some trivia question. "Urgent call for you in the office."

Sister Roberta had always hated me.

"Hello?"

Peggy's voice was a siren wailing down Van Ness. "Get home now, Frances."

I'd left my backpack in social studies but had my bike keys in my pocket. I put the phone down, didn't even look up at Sister Roberta. I dropped my hall pass on the desk, sprinted out of the office and down the long fluorescent-lit hall, through the double doors and out to the bicycle rack. Unlock the clunker and pedal. Those hilly streets never felt like such mountains.

Bent over the white-sheeted hospital bed, Peggy had her ear to Nana's mouth. "We got her back," she said, breathless. "She was down for the count."

Peggy could have been such a volleyball coach.

Nana moaned something as I took her fleshy hand.

"The ambulances in this city are a joke," Peggy mumbled. "I called ten minutes ago."

"He's not coming," Nana whispered, pale and confused.

"Who's not coming, Nana?"

Peggy adjusted the blankets covering her feet.

"Our Lord," Nana whispered. She didn't open her eyes. "He promised . . ."

"It's okay, Nana. I'm here."

Her breath heavied. She opened her mouth, pushed the words out. "There's no one here."

After all those years of penance and prayer, God, of crossing herself and confessing, of churchgoing and rosary-bead counting, of cake baking and tithing that ridiculous chunk of our Social Security check, of Hail Marys and mea culpas, would it have been so damn much trouble for you to send someone to meet her? Maybe Jesus was busy—fair enough—any obscure old saint would have done.

"No one," my grandmother whispered.

And here's the worst part, God: Even in that moment of heartbreak and abandonment, she probably forgave you. On her deathbed, my Nana forgave you. How come you never have to feel guilty, God?

Teresa of Avila

(IF YOU NEED DIRECT CONTACT)

A.K.A. The Roving Nun

FEAST DAY: October 15

SYMBOLS: a pierced heart, a book, a dove

For years, Teresa of Avila suffered poor health—probably malaria—an unpleasant prayer life, major guilt pangs, and debilitating shame spirals.

When she complained to God about it all, he just said, "Teresa, so do I treat my friends."

"That's why you have so few friends," she snapped.

Still, she remained devoted.

As a young teen, Teresa had lost her mom. Nine kids left to a single dad. It was time for the girl to figure out what she intended to do with her life: matrimony or the convent? Marriage prospects weren't that great for the Christian descendant of a Jew in sixteenth-century Spain, and Teresa managed to dim them further by having an affair. She entered a convent for the first time at age eighteen—but just as a boarder. After less than two years, ill health forced her to return home.

Her father didn't want her to leave again. "Find a man," he said. "Any man."

She found plenty of men, but none of them husband material. The pickings were just too slim. Nights of passion, but by morning she was over it. It was under cover of darkness that Teresa ran away to the Carmelite Convent of the Incarnation. But the religious community turned out to be something less than pure. Rich nuns kept servants and lapdogs, lived in private suites, wore jewelry and perfume. Poor sisters slept in a dorm. They all had plenty of male visitors.

Teresa's malaria started acting up again—fevers and fainting spells—so the mother superior packed her up once more and released her to her dad. She was given experimental treatments and quack cures, got worse. Finally her dad brought her home to die.

"My tongue was bitten to pieces," she later wrote. "Nothing had passed my lips and because of this and of my great weakness my throat was choking me so that I could not even take water. All my bones seemed to be out of joint and there was a terrible confusion in my head. As a result of the torments I had suffered during these days, I was all doubled up, like a ball, and no more able to move arm, foot, hand, or head than if I had been dead."

She fell into a coma, was given last rites. Her grave was dug, her coffin left open. She would have been buried, but her dad kept insisting: "She isn't dead yet."

When she woke up, she couldn't open her eyes—they'd already been sealed shut with wax in preparation for burial.

For months, Teresa lay paralyzed, but it was during this time that she took to daily mental prayer. She insisted on being taken back to the convent, where she remained in the infirmary for several years, recovering in time to nurse her dad through his own final illness. "I felt as if my own soul was being torn out of me, for I loved him much," she wrote. "He died like an angel."

In time, the passion she'd turned toward the various men in her life became focused on Christ, who appeared to her in her cell—the most sacred Humanity in full beauty and majesty.

She spent long hours in meditation, often slipped into trances where she felt her soul lifted out of her body like a "detachable death." Her mystical flights were disorienting to Teresa—even embarrassing—but they were also dangerous. It wasn't uncommon for visionaries to wind up at the stake. Some sisters and friends shunned her, afraid of being associated with a witch. Her autobiography was already being examined by the Inquisition for signs of heresy. *The granddaughter of a Jew who claims to see angels?*

"I do not fear Satan half so much as I fear those who fear him," she said.

Her raptures continued. When she was forty-four years old, a cherub appeared to Teresa, its face aflame. When it plunged a golden spear into her heart, she moaned in agony, didn't want it to stop. From that moment, she vowed to live only for God.

Despite tremendous opposition within the Carmelite order, she got permission from Rome to found a strict convent in Avila. No jewelry or lapdogs there. Her nuns lived in quiet and poverty. No table or chair graced Teresa's small cell. She wrote kneeling on the floor under a window. She didn't reread her work, and she did no editing.

Bathed in rays of brilliant gold, she likened prayer to a garden, made it sound almost simple: Step 1 is meditation—slow and laborious, like drawing water from a deep well by hand. Step 2 is simple quiet—you still your senses so your soul can begin to receive guidance. More water is drawn, but less energy is expended. Your attachments to earthly things begin to fall away. Step 3 is union—no-stress contact with God. It's as if a little spring has bubbled up and the garden becomes self-watering. Step 4—well, step 4 is done by God herself, raining from above. You faint into a swoon of perfect receptivity.

After Teresa died at the age of sixty-seven, a heavenly scent permeated her tomb. When her body was exhumed, it was sweet smelling and incorrupt. Pieces were amputated as relics. Her heart, hands, right foot, right arm, left eye, and part of her jaw are on display at various sites around the world.

If you suffer from headaches, fear heart attack, or long for a direct line to God, invoke the Roving Nun. Build a simple altar with a heart, an arrow, and a book. Follow the steps and cultivate the garden. Be gentle to all, and stern with yourself. Say thanks to Teresa by testing the limits of faith and authority. And when things get rough, repeat after the earthy mystic: *Let nothing disturb thee, let nothing affright thee. All things are passing. God alone abideth.*

I slip my T- shirt back on, dry now, but not my jeans, and crawl to the edge of my granite hill.

The little boy below has a huge hammock of a net, wears nothing but a pair of Spider-Man underwear. He attaches one end of his hammock to a tree stump near the water's edge, swims with the other end in his fist as he sings.

I watch his wide arc.

"Gotchaaaa!" he cries, grabbing a flapping silver fish from his net and running through the water with it like it's a home-run baseball. He drops it into a plastic bag hanging from the branch of a pine tree and he's back in the water.

I miss Manny something fierce—his bellowing songs, his bright morning face.

"I come from Alabama!" the little boy yells. "With a big ol' banjo on my knee!" He seems as pleased when he doesn't catch a fish as when he does.

"Son?" a low voice calls through the trees.

The boy darts from the water, rushes for his bag. "I caught a fish, Dad! I caught one!"

A rustling of pine needles.

I wait on the rock as father and child break down their tent and pack up with their fish. When I'm pretty sure the coast is clear, I make my way down from my sunny perch, wade into the lagoon to inspect the old hammock net the boy left. It's got a few big holes in it, but I tie them off. I hold the unanchored end of the net, follow the little boy's arc through the blue chill. A small school approaching, I splash-run to snag them, trip over a slimy rock. None of the fish catch in my net. I shake my head at the fates. *If a seven-year-old singing "Oh, Susanna" can catch a fish, why not me?* I rock-hop back to the beginning of his arc, pull my net through the lagoon again and again. "Oh, Susanna," I start to sing, "don't you cry for me!" But it's hopeless. A half dozen silver fish approach, sniffing at my stupid net. I grab both sides, pull it fast around them, but the fish just scatter like shadows. They're not stupid. Me, on the other hand—I'm dumb as a bag of marshmallows. I want to cry. The afternoon sun is sinking in the sky and my net is empty. I'm famished. I could make myself bleed I'm so damn hungry, but who would come to my rescue?

It occurs to me that my trick is kind of passive-aggressive.

I bend to my knees, the lake-bottom gravel rough against my skin. "Fish," I say, "it's true I'm trying to kill you, but, see, Dorothy's expecting quite a few people tonight and just between you and me I'm gonna venture that she doesn't get much company up here. What I'm saying is that if you'll let me catch you, I'll be crazy-grateful and I swear I won't let anyone waste a bite."

With that Anthony of Padua probably could've caught a whole yellow boatload of fish—153 of 'em, maybe—but me, I flail around in the water, careening between clumsiness and near-injury for what must be another two sloshing hours before I catch—*yes I do!*—three fat rainbow trout in my beautiful holy string hammock net.

"Thank you, fish!" My words echo off the old volcano mountain. "Thank you, fish!"

I tie the net up at the edge of the water so the fish are still submerged even though they're entrapped, and I wade into the deep—in the direction of my sunken wine. Plunge into the indigo depth. Locating the jugs is easy enough, they're right in the sand where they fell, but when I dive down and hook two fingers through the first jug's handle and pull, it's like trying to lift a boulder. Bubbles from my nose. I need air. I drop the jug, somersault up, and kick back to the surface, gasping.

I tread water, getting a few good breaths, then dive in again, manage to pull the jug to shallower water before I drop it again. Third time down, and I've got the first jug in two hands. I drag it to the shore, set it in the grass next to my boat, which still needs patching. Back out into the blue. I'm getting used to the glacial temperature, wonder if this is how people catch pneumonia—by adjusting to zero.

Whoever thought I'd bust my ass like this for two jugs of Gallo?

Fully dressed again, I circle the island, but the closest thing to boat-patch I can find is a handful of bark and needles, some sap I manage to scrape from a pine's shaded wound. "Thanks," I whisper to the tree. The sap softens a little in my hand as I make my way back to my boat.

I cover the hole best I can with the sap and tree mixture. My idea is that it'll harden in the cold water. Get us home, anyway. Strange to think of Dorothy's one-room cabin as home, but that's where we're headed—me and my three fish trailing the canoe in their hammock net.

Less than halfway to my docking spot, cool water starts to seep into the wooden boat. We can't go down here, the lake's too deep. I could swim to the shore easily enough, but not with the wine and fish. *I'm not giving up my wine and fish now.*

I climb-roll out of the boat, careful not to tip it, wet jeans heavy on my body.

The dusky shore is all that matters now. My fish flap fins like they want to help push the boat for the little cabin— either that or they've changed their minds and want their freedom.

I roll the yellow canoe over onto the grassy turf shore, go running up to the cabin for Dorothy's blue bucket.

"All right, trout." I ease them from their net and into the water-filled bucket. "Listen. I'm planning to kill you, then wrap you and cook you in the fire, you got that?"

The fish chase each other's tails, circling in their tiny plastic lake as I carry them up to the cabin.

My pine nuts and thyme are wet in my pocket, but I dump them out onto the table next to the bucket.

Outside, I gather twigs, wonder what time it's getting to be. Days seem to last so much longer up here, sun inching across the sky. It's not that a girl can get much done—all the hours of light consumed just trying to put together some paltry sustenance—but it feels like a lifetime since I woke, sore boned and staring incredulous at Dorothy in the doorway.

Chapter 18
TAKE AND EAT

A funny thing happened when Saint Patrick crashed a Druid's party back in fifth-century Ireland.

"Okay, saint boy, let's see what you're made of," one of the elders said under his breath as he handed the uninvited guest a cup of poisoned wine.

When Patrick raised the cup to the light, the poison rose to the surface. He blew it off, then toasted everyone in good cheer.

But that's another story.

✝

Dorothy's guests arrive solo and in pairs. Dusty, long-haired Sierra hermits and hoboes in secondhand work pants take their places at the humble table I've set with mismatched dishes and glowing beeswax candles.

An old man grips a fiddle in his calloused hand.

A woman carries a fistful of lavender.

Gray-haired Isabel, my ride up from the bus shelter, holds a bottle of red wine. "I see you found your way," she winks.

No need for miracles now, just Dorothy's sun-reddened friends and everything begins to multiply. Someone's brought bright orange flowers he says we can eat, so I place a blossom on each small square of campfire-cooked fish.

A woman with a thousand braids offers a bag of apricots. "Dessert!"

My jeans still haven't dried, so I've wrapped a found red sheet around my waist, figure I'll call it a skirt.

The worn wooden "Hospitality" sign on Dorothy's door, and who knew I'd be the host? I pour wine into mugs, glasses, and Sierra cups, offer rounds of herbed fry bread and flowered fish.

"Catch this today?" someone asks.

"A few hours ago," I brag.

"I've been a vegetarian for twenty years," the guy grumbles. Bearded hobo.

I swallow hard, thinking of my dancing trout. They gave their lives for this dinner. *What if the whole lot of them are vegetarians?*

But the old guy just scoops up a forkful of fish and brings it to his chapped lips like some kind of delicacy. He chews slowly. "Damn good," he says. "This'll hold me for another twenty."

Cheers.

A young guy with a scruffy goatee has a gift for Dorothy. Darting eyes, he reminds me of someone who once gave me bus fare when it was raining.

Dorothy peels away the green tissue paper, careful not to tear it. Inside, a hand-knit brown wool sweater.

"I hope you're not going to give it away," the guy says.

Dorothy shrugs, running her hand over the wool. "It's beautiful, Gerald."

One of the old hermits is talking about UFOs that hover near his campsite up at Shealor Lake in the earliest hours.

"Do the Martians talk to you?" someone wants to know.

"Yep," he nods. His eyebrows are manzanita bushes. "They tell me the glory of this nation'll fade right before my eyes as we're attacked from inside and out. But they tell me they'll save the world on the brink of doomsday. That's when they'll land, huh. Twenty-twelve."

"Armageddon?" someone else pipes up.

But the old hermit shakes his head. "Not like the one you're thinkin' of. Holographic energy . . ."

"What's in the bread?" Isabel wants to know.

Exactly everything I found in the cupboard plus the pine nuts and thyme, but Dorothy answers for me: "A city girl's best intentions."

I'd never thought of myself as a city girl before I met Dorothy, but I guess it's true. I'm far off the interstate now.

"To the sweetest ingredient of all," she toasts.

More wine.

Old man fiddle, arms covered in fading prison tattoos, lifts his instrument from its black case, resins up his bow, and starts to play a quick bluegrass tune.

The woman with a thousand braids excuses herself to the outhouse.

The wine courses through my veins like some kind of electricity.

"Are you expecting anyone else?" the woman wants to know when she comes back inside. "There's some European guy out on the ridge. Claims to be looking for one Frances Catherine."

A flash of anxiety.

The fiddler finishes his song.

All eyes on me.

"Don't tell him I'm in here" is all I say, but he's already standing in the doorway. Barbaro. "How did you find me?"

Isabel hums.

Dorothy rises, hand outstretched. "What she meant to say was, 'Welcome.' "

Barbaro hesitates.

"There's plenty of food," the vegetarian offers.

I want to slap him.

Barbaro's got stubble on his chin, mud on his red corduroy pants, looks like some young Grizzly Adams stumbling in from the wilderness, disoriented. "I am grateful that I found you," he says. Salty water wells up in his eyes, but no tears fall.

Isabel pours him a mug full of wine. "Yes, welcome!"

The fiddler starts up again, this time bowing a slow country tune.

I can hardly look at Barbaro. My shame and indignation, my sorrow and dread, all mixed up into some sour brew.

Dorothy points him to the empty chair, the extra plate of food she served for no apparent reason.

"Thank you," he says. He sits down, takes a few hungry bites, then turns to me. "I came to speak with you, Frankka."

Obviously.

I can feel my cheeks redden.

The fiddler plays on.

What business does Barbaro have, showing up here and crashing my hospitality party? "Then speak," I say, teeth clenched. They've sent him up here to find me because they know I'm a sucker for his dumb accent, his dumb trust in life. I count my betrayers on both hands under the table: All my fellow travelers. The old minister, surely. Isabel, maybe. Even Dorothy. Where did she have to go today? Who did she tell that I'd come? *You are about to be manipulated,* I tell myself. *Send up the wall.*

Barbaro clears his throat. "I would prefer to speak alone."

I'm sure he would. I shake my head no, look him right in the eye, my invisible wall now firmly erected. "Talk to me here or just enjoy your dinner and forget it," I snap. I feel like such a dolt, sitting here playing out some city girl soap opera script for all the friendly hoboes and mountain freaks. I can't tell from their candlelit faces if they're amused or annoyed. I don't know which reaction I'd consider more embarrassing. All I wanted was for them to swoon over my fish and fried bread. All I wanted was for them to accept me like some long-lost member of their *famiglia*. All I wanted was to please Dorothy.

"It was neither Magdelena nor Pia who betrayed you," Barbaro announces.

So they've sent him up here to feed me lies, to convince me of their innocence. I guess the fiddler likes the theater of it all, because he plays with long, melodramatic strokes now.

"How can you know that?" I ask Barbaro, stone-faced.

He looks down at his food, then back to me. "I know because I am the one who told everything."

"Uh-oh," Isabel hums.

My wall starts to crumble, like sand. Quick inhale. *Keep it up. Reinforce.*

Silence. Forks frozen midair.

"Well, well," the woman with a thousand braids finally says. "Welcome, stranger."

I manage a smile, excuse myself from the table. My humiliation tastes like buttermilk. Nowhere to go in a one-room cabin, so I step out onto the porch, make my way down the steps.

Standing alone under more stars than I ever knew existed, the drama queen in me would have Barbaro come rushing on my heels, begging forgiveness and professing his buried love. The little girl waiting for her parents wants Mama Dorothy to come flying, arms outstretched. The hostess who only wants a family waits for them all to file out after me, *famiglia* from scratch. But I just stumble alone in the dark toward the shore, the black lake spread out before me like a headache. I could jump into this cold and swim, refuse to come up for air until I saw the face of eternity. I could open my arms to the heavens, offer myself as a victim to God's merciful love, wait for the fiery darts to pierce my heart. A coyote cries from a snowcapped mountain.

I can hear the fiddler inside, playing a quickening song.

The clink of glasses, conversation rising and falling.

What does Barbaro mean, *he* told? It doesn't make any sense. He's lying, but why? He's covering for Magdelena. Or maybe I'm already dead.

"Frankka?" It's Barbaro's voice from the porch. "Frankka, you are out here?"

A dog howls from some separate shore.

"Frankka?"

"Stop yelling, Barbaro."

He shuffles down the dirt trail, stands in the starlight blowing no flames. "Our fellow travelers feel so sad and broken," he says. "I am myself a hollow man." He wrings his hands. "I am honest when I tell you I believed Judy to be sincere in her curiosity. I explained to her the need for secrecy and security under these unusual circumstances. I believed she only wanted to know this road show as I do."

I'm not buying a word of it. "So you broke into my room? You let her draw my blood? Or maybe you did it yourself. You guys screwed me over. And that's one thing, but now there are a bunch of other people out there who think we're either saviors or Satans—they either think I'm some mystical healer or they want to burn me at the stake. We're screwed. Magdelena completely screwed us over."

Lonely hollow man. I remember the way he stood on that night in Yellow Springs, snow falling in his hair, hopeful-excited, auditioning for *The Death & Resurrection Show* he knew was his destiny. He says, "I only betrayed to Judy your secret. I did not help her with any evidence or photography. We have all spoken about this, and we do not believe she obtained any blood sample. We feel this to be a lie. Magdelena has also made a mistake. That night after our beautiful performance in Lincoln City, do you remember? That night we shared drinks with Judy and believed the interviews to be over, yet she did ask Magdelena to share a cigarette in your room. Now Magdelena can remember, she believes, she is almost certain, she knows now, that at some moment she may have excused herself to the toilet to make a pee. Perhaps in this moment Judy made a photograph of your hand."

It's getting cold out here. My *Sesame Street* T-shirt and red sheet a joke against the night chill, but I feel weirdly calm. I say, "Barbaro, I loved you that night in Yellow Springs when you stood out in the snow, and I would never love anyone so stupid as to think an *L.A. Times* reporter could keep a secret. So, if you're not stupid, that only leaves two possibilities: You're either lying or you're a real asshole." I look up for the moon, but all I can see is Magdelena's pale face in the sky. I'm an asshole, too, I know, but I don't say that.

Barbaro speaks softly. "I have come to ask you to return to our troupe. We need you, Frankka. I cannot know if you will choose to do so. In any case, I have also brought you your share of the ticket sales from Sacramento and San Francisco. Some refunds had to be given to those who only came to see you, but your share is still one thousand dollars."

"Even though I bailed?"

"We all decided it was fair that I should bring you the money."

"A bribe?"

Barbaro shakes his head. "We have made an error, Frankka."

I don't ask how the shows went. I've often thought that my part, although central, could easily be written out. Magdelena's flight alone could carry the show. Who'd know the difference? But those people in Sacramento and San Francisco had come for blood. I say, "I don't know how you found me, Barbaro, or why you came all this way, but you've made your confession, right? Now go back. I was having a nice dinner."

"Yes. I will go."

★   ★   ★

Back inside the cabin, no one mentions Barbaro's arrival or departure. We eat halved apricots as the conversation wanes. "Another glass of wine?"

"You look cold," Dorothy says, offering me her new hand-knit sweater. I slip it over my head.

Chapter 19
GRIEF

After my Nana died, days felt like trying to push bricks through tunnels.

When the black telephone in the kitchen rang, I answered in a mumble.

I hardly recognized my maternal grandmother's voice on the other end. She'd called to tell me that I could come live with her and Grandpa Joe in their pristine blue tract house outside Denver. "You're always welcome here," she said.

I stood there, phone in hand, silent. How many years had I waited to hear those words? How many times had I fantasized that the weeks I'd spent with them the summer after first grade stretched into a lifetime? How many nights had I stayed awake, envisioning myself as one of those clean-cut suburban kids playing in the park at the end of their cul-de-sac?

For that two-week trip to Colorado, I'd packed only my cleanest corduroys and prettiest flowered blouses, but Grandma

Jeanie picked through my Mighty Mouse suitcase and shook her head. "Let's go to the shopping center and find something you can wear to church, dear."

At JC Penney, she bought me a brand-new pink dress with scratchy lace around the collar, white tights, black patent leather Mary Janes. She paid with a credit card.

In the morning, I sat through their Protestant mass, which wasn't called a mass, wiggled my toes in my new shoes, bowed my head like it all made sense.

At home in the blue tract house, I watched golf on television with Grandpa Joe. A giant crystal bowl of wrapped coffee candy tempted me from the table between us, but I never took one.

Over a dinner of lamb chops, mashed potatoes, and boiled carrots, I unfolded my cloth napkin only after Grandpa Joe had unfolded his, and I smoothed the white linen square across my lap, imagining what a nice granddaughter they'd think I was.

I spoke only when spoken to and made my bed. I emptied the dishwasher without being asked. I never left my dolls on the floor.

Did I look like my mother?

But Grandma Jeanie never mentioned my mother, and Grandpa Joe cleared his throat and changed the subject when I asked him if this was the house she'd grown up in.

The last morning there at the breakfast table, a bowl of Grape-Nuts in front of me, I sipped my Sunny Delight, waited for an opening.

Grandma Jeanie smiled, tapped a manicured nail on the wooden table. "I'll bet you're looking forward to seeing all of your friends at home, aren't you, dear?"

But I wasn't looking forward to seeing the fly-children. I set down my juice cup at the upper right hand corner of my yellow placemat where it belonged and piped up, "I would very much like to come and live here with you in Colorado."

Grandpa Joe folded his newspaper over, looked at Grandma Jeanie.

I sat up straight, held-breath hopeful.

Grandma Jeanie smiled at me. "Well, dear, maybe we can talk to your Nana about that."

"Oh, my Nana wouldn't mind at all," I promised. "It's real hard work for her, taking care of me. I mean . . ." I regretted saying the thing about hard work right away. "I won't be any trouble for you. I promise. It's just hard for her because . . ." I trailed off. "I won't be any trouble at all."

Grandma Jeanie held her smile. "Of course you wouldn't be any trouble, dear."

I bit my lip. "Will you call her now?"

"Soon, dear." Grandma Jeanie nodded slowly. "Well. We'd better get you packed up."

Of course. Packed up. I'd have to go back to my Nana's to get the rest of my things.

At home in our San Francisco apartment, I whispered in the bathroom mirror, "I'm from Colorado," and smiled the way I imagined girls from Colorado smiled. I could see my future clearly: my suburban life, the giant public school halfway between my grandparents' house and JC Penney. Sunny Delight and shopping center church.

Grandma Jeanie would call my Nana soon, tell her I was no trouble at all.

What is "soon" exactly? A week? A month? Maybe a season? Easter, when you thought about it, could be classified as "soon."

We changed our clocks back and we changed our clocks forward, but the black telephone didn't ring. Cards came on holidays picturing lazy cartoon cats and pink flowers. *Thinking of You, Granddaughter,* and checks for twenty-five dollars. I sent my thank-you notes on time, but Grandma Jeanie and Grandpa Joe never invited me back to their blue tract house outside Denver.

Now Grandma Jeanie's voice sounded like an old woman's. "You've been through so much, dear."

But it was too late. Maybe she knew it was too late—maybe that's why she offered. What would I do in Colorado now? My orphan's Social Security check wouldn't go away just because my Nana was gone. Seven months 'til graduation, my application already out to the University of California. "I'll be fine here," I promised.

"All right, dear, but you know our door is always open."

It's amazing, when you think about it, what grief can do to people.

Chapter 20

CONFESSION

Maybe I've had too much to drink, or maybe silence can only sustain itself for so long, but as I clear the table and rinse the dinner dishes in the blue bucket of lake water on the porch, I have the urge to tell Dorothy everything.

I wipe down the table. Just one candle still burns.

I sit across from her, wait a long time before I break the spell of quiet.

Dorothy sits statue-still as I tell her about the way I never stuck up for Ezekiel Goldstein against the fly-children who swarmed on the schoolyard at All Saints K–8, how I cheated on my tests, letting the saints whisper the answers in my ears and then taking credit like I'd studied all along. I tell her how I never touched the tomb at Assisi, that it was all a lie, and how I only made friends in high school after I learned to gossip. I admit that I've always been a little bit jealous of Magdelena—the ease with which she seemed to glide through life, her social grace, her absolute trust in her catcher. And I tell her how I've always felt a little bit superior to Madre Pia, seeing as I'd long since figured out that God was an asshole and she, even after being born the wrong sex, didn't seem to have a clue. I admit that I thought Dorothy herself was kind of a loser in her housedress and comfortable shoes, and that I'd cursed all the way to the garbage dump from behind the grocery store/tackle shop. I tell her about the time I stole the book on Christian symbolism from the punk house in Austin, no intention of returning it, stole from Magdelena the very camisole I now wore under my *Sesame Street* T-shirt. I tell her about Sacramento and the way my anger bubbled up from some unknown pit and spat blame at my fellow travelers. I tell her about the way I wanted to kill Magdelena in my dream, and how I faked the stigmata as a child, identifying not at all with the suffering of Christ. I tell her that I hadn't really learned to fish at all this afternoon— that I'd begged those rainbow trout to let me catch them. When I'm done, the thick silence descends again and I don't know what I'm waiting for, exactly, in the flickering candlelight. Absolution? Some prescription for 108 Hail Marys punctuated by a few Our Fathers?

When Dorothy opens her mouth, she has no recipe for my penance. "What do you think a saint is?" she asks. "Some kind of perfect person? Errorless? Someone who sacrifices themselves and makes the right choice for the greater good every chance they get? *Read* the lives of the saints. Every last one of them was flawed, scarred, quirky. They heard voices. They didn't look great in their bathing suits. They had hair in the wrong places. They weren't gods, Frankka, they were seekers like you and me. But they came to understand their destinies. I'm not saying you should try to be a saint—who wants to be dismissed that easily? But don't imagine that your past needs to dictate your future. Do you remember Pavlov's dogs?"

"Sure," I nod. "They were conditioned to salivate at the sound of a bell."

"When a flood submerged Pavlov's laboratory, not one of the surviving dogs retained a trace of its conditioning. Think about that." Dorothy stands. "Will you be leaving to rejoin your troupe tomorrow?"

"Don't you get it?" I say. "I can't rejoin my troupe. I'm a fraud."

She picks up the little tray of leftovers, carries them toward the door. She pauses at the threshold, turns to me, suddenly stern. "No, Frankka," she says. "You're worse than a fraud. You're the real thing pretending to be a fraud."

I take a single wool blanket from the cot I've been sleeping on, carry it out to the porch, down the wooden stairs, and across the soft ground to the flat granite rock at the lake's edge.

Barbaro says my troupe needs me. I don't believe him. But it's true that I've been mourning something these last few days in the mountains. The loss of my fellow travelers, maybe, but more than that, I'm hungry for the stage. Each night when that last curtain fell on *The Death & Resurrection Show*, I stood in the dark and my performance grabbed me by the wrists, shook me hard, demanded an explanation for every way in which I'd failed it: the theatrical pause that should have stretched longer, the over- or underexpressiveness I'd managed to improvise in that circle of friends, the magic I came so close to imparting. *Communication.*

It's strange to realize that that's what I've been after all these years—some kind of pure symbolic communication, like the images in a child's mind, uncluttered by the rules of semantics and polite society. If language was meaningless without a shared context, there had to be another way to connect. An exchange that could bypass the maze of rational interpretation. A Latin of the soul, maybe, mysterious and unknowable yet miraculously comprehended. There had to be, but even after my very best shows, when that revelation of transcendent spirit seemed to rise exquisite from my shoulders, I was left in the dark, shaken. I hadn't quite done it. So I returned to the stage, implored by my own performance there behind the curtain to make that final leap. Reviewers in zines and local papers praised my act, the audience cheered—*hallelujah!*—but it wasn't the audience of people I wanted to reach, was it? No, I meant to communicate with an invisible world. With God.

I sit at the lake's edge, no audience but the stars, and I try to remember Teresa of Avila's vision of the interior life. A seven-roomed castle cut from a single diamond. A doorway made of meditation and prayer.

"Many souls remain in the outer court of the castle, which is the place occupied by the guards," Teresa cautioned. "They are not interested in entering it, and have no idea what there is in that wonderful place, or who dwells in it, or even how many rooms it has."

I close my eyes, steady my breath. The castle is vast, glistening. *How long has it been since I've entered this place?* From the doorway, I can already see some of the rooms. In the center of it all lives the Divine Essence—union with the creator. In that inner room, the most secret things can pass between soul and God, between God and soul. *But what are the other rooms a girl has to go through to get there?* Humility, yes. Quiet and illumination. Self-knowledge. The Dark Night of shame and doubt and emptiness.

"The important thing is not to think much," Teresa said, "but to love much; do, then, whatever most arouses you to love."

Chapter 21

WHO WOULDN'T DIE?

Sunrise at a newsstand in Stockton. I pay a dollar for the *L.A. Times,* scan the news and lifestyle sections for any word of my hysterical hypochondria, but it's all plane crashes and celebrity divorces, hurricanes and body counts. Thirteen soldiers killed in a faraway desert. The Dow Jones Industrial Average slipping. Maybe it's just like the old minister said: *They'll be on to somethin' else by next week—ferget all aboutcha.* A single smiling face glows in black and white from below the fold, a brief story about Clowns Without Borders sending performers and doctors to a refugee camp at the edge of the war zone. I tear the story out carefully, slip the newsprint smile into my back pocket. The events section of the paper carries the only mention of *The Death & Resurrection Show: One night only, 7 P.M., Hermosa Beach Playhouse.* I've never heard of the venue, but I pour nickels into a pay phone, call the listed number. *For a calendar of events, press 1; for tickets, press 2; to book a show, press 3.* I want a human, so I try 0, am surprised when it works.

"Sold out, dude," the human tells me.

"But the show's going on?"

"Sure. It's not, like, *canceled*. Got moved down here 'cause the café in Santa Monica couldn't handle it, but if you're looking for that bleeding chick, she's the no-show. Got freaked out about all the buzz. Pretty trippy. I mean, who wouldn't die to get their picture on the front page of the *L.A. Times?*"

"People are weird," I tell him.

"Yeah. Pretty weird. Anyway, dude. Like I said, sold out."

The 9:35 A.M. Greyhound to L.A. isn't sold out. Costs $44, so I peel a few twenties from the wad Barbaro left me, still not sure if I'm doing the right thing. Every day I ask for signs, but every day God hangs silent.

Maybe it's like the kids at UC Santa Cruz used to tell me—that we shouldn't look for a supreme being in the clouds but trust that God lives in us all. Should I be worshiping myself because I'm a part of it? *Anytime you want to, let me know, God.*

The bus smells like fast food grease and that's not a sign of anything but America. A half dozen lonely teenagers stare out windows, and I imagine they're following Highway 5 south like it's some yellow brick road to Hollywood stardom. Who knows, maybe it is. Maybe they'll get their pictures on the front page of the *L.A. Times* without dying. But I always worry about kids who haven't lost their beauty yet—worry about who'll try to steal it and if they'll survive the crime.

I take my seat near the back of the bus, drift off easily and jerk awake. We pass the vast slaughterhouse near Tracy, the smell of manure and death. I drift off and jerk awake. Hours of barren yellow, no bricks. I'm holding a mason jar of Sierra wildflowers in my lap, a couple inches of lake water to keep them alive. Dorothy insisted I take Gerald's brown knit sweater for the journey, too—woman can't keep a gift, apparently—but the morning chill has already blown off, so I'm holding that, too. I need to find a Laundromat or some new clothes in L.A. One or the other. I wonder who's got my duffel—if anyone's got my duffel. I want my saint book back. I've been scrawling myself stories on paper napkins and in my head, and there's only so much of that a girl can do before she starts feeling orphaned and homeless. I drift off and I'm somewhere else entirely. Uniformed guards line a white wall. California has enacted a voluntary death penalty. Barbaro and I wait in line for our chance to sit in the electric chair. A white-bearded old veteran rants as they strap him in. The currents charge through him and his body jolts, then goes limp. *Next.* A tantruming little boy cries, stomping his feet. Barbaro and I exchange a quick glance. We've changed our minds. We grab the baby and leave, go swimming at a red clay–banked river in Humboldt County. I jerk awake.

The guy sitting next to me smells of turpentine.

"Morning," I mumble.

He doesn't look at me. "Pretty well afternoon by now," he says.

★   ★   ★

At the station in L.A., I can already see the creeping disappointment on the teenage runaways' faces. Just a bus station in some seedy neighborhood that in so many ways might as well be Stockton. I smile as I pass them. *What more can I do?* They're still too aloof to accept help, to even know they might need it. What could I offer them, anyway, beyond a nod of good luck? I make my way out into the balmy afternoon alone.

Los Angeles: I've always secretly loved this city. This Black White Asian Native city that should have stayed part of Mexico. The fake tans covered in sunscreen and the traffic jams made of off-road vehicles. The odd geography of desert meeting ocean. The smoggy light dusting everything with tragedy-tinged enchantment. Makes me thirsty.

I have to take two Metro trains and a bus to get where I'm going. "About an hour," the guy at the station told me. I figure he means two. I've been through L.A. often enough to know the residents can't handle their own congestion, are forced to lie about it just to maintain sanity. Even so, it's only four o'clock. L.A. denial accounted for, and I've still got plenty of time.

I'm getting hungry, but I just buy a bottle of Calistoga water and some sugar-free gum from a corner kiosk.

At a dumb boutique where headless mannequins wear yellow miniskirts, the saleswoman fawns over me. "Oh, honey, you need something to show off your figure!" I can't tell how old she is because the muscles in her face are frozen like she's had a stroke or too many antiwrinkle injections, but I can tell she's disappointed when I choose a long white cotton sari dress with pants to go underneath. "Your *figure*," she whines.

Ferget all aboutcha.

On the Metro train, I stare at an old Latino guy across the aisle, am convinced I recognize him from some eighties sit-com, but I can't quite put my finger on it.

"What the hell you looking at?" he finally asks.

On the bus, I watch out the window, trying to mind my own business. The vining bougainvillea and flowering jacaranda trees; snaking traffic at the end of the continent.

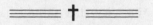

I remember a rainy night in Tacoma. Madre had family in the area, sent her parents and grandparents yellow-flowered invitations to our 7:00 P.M. show.

She'd said she didn't think they'd come, shrugged it off, but she waited in the wings, peering out from behind the curtain as our small audience filed in. Usually strict about getting the show started on time, she said, "Let's wait another ten minutes, people might be running late with the storm."

At 7:30 she finally lowered the lights and took to the stage, dejected. "In the beginning God created the heavens and the earth . . ."

When Barbaro fed me my beet red juice and I stood, resurrected, Madre rose from behind me.

A sudden boozy voice from the darkness: "That's my boy!"

Tears streamed down Madre's face, streaking her makeup pale under the lights as she rose.

After the show, Madre changed into corduroys and a man's dress shirt, and we took her grandfather out to play pool at Hell's Kitchen.

Pia didn't ask about the rest of her family, but her grandfather explained anyway: "Simple ignorance," he said. He patted Madre on the back. "You do a damn fine show, son."

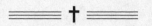

The Hermosa Beach Playhouse looks more like a public school than a theater, a big concrete building squared by southern California palms, but the marquee advertises my stop clearly in red letters:

— Tonight Only —

THE DEATH & RESURRECTION SHOW

I nod my thanks to the driver, step off into the blue flame of late afternoon. I make my way across the wet lawn toward what looks like a main entrance, careful not to disturb the sleeping wino in my path. On the corner, two protesters argue with each other, one holding a sign that says "Jesus Loves You," the other wearing a giant crucifix and yelling "Repent!" But they don't seem to notice me.

The box office isn't open yet, so I just creep in through heavy doors.

From the darkness of the back of the house, I watch my fellow travelers unfurl the indigo backdrop, position platforms onstage. Paula rigs the ropes and swings with the help of a slim woman I've never seen before. *Have I already been replaced?* Tony tests his amp, serious-methodical. Lupe rushes across the stage, then back again, preoccupied. Barbaro sits crouched in the corner, fidgeting with his carnival mask. They don't need me. I could tiptoe out of here so easily, get back on the bus, and just keep going. Anything in motion desires to stay in motion. The show would go on. But who ever cheated fate by running away?

══════ † ══════

I remember the first time all seven of us performed together. Must have been a couple of weeks after we left Baltimore. We'd gotten waylaid in a thin-walled motel room in the middle of a December storm that knocked down power lines and stranded travelers up and down the eastern seaboard and into the Midwest.

"Where ya going in such shit for weather?" the motel guy asked as I headed out on foot. "Crazy," he muttered.

But if you never walk through a blizzard, you'll never know how much heat the human body emits. I trudged down the icy highway in search of provisions and a plastic Christmas tree covered in tinsel. The single open minimart making a killing in the storm.

Back in our crowded motel room, we drank blackstrap rum from the bottle and ate black-eyed peas from the can, decorated our fake tree with Manny's LEGOs.

Manny worried that Santa wouldn't make it through the blizzard, and Lupe tried to convince us all to lie to the child about the date. He was so little yet—*How would he know if we postponed Christmas for a week?* But we couldn't agree to the hoax, and Saint Nick and those reindeer are no weather wimps. They flew through the sky and down into our chimneyless room, bringing Manny a Curious George doll and a shiny red fire truck. Madre Pia got a snow globe with a nun in it, and Paula a green and black flask. Barbaro scored a copy of *The Smile at the Foot of the Ladder,* and Magdelena got clover honey and a feather boa. For Tony there were red and black striped socks, and for Lupe, a conch shell so she could listen to the ocean. As for me, Santa saw fit to wrap up a gaudy copper crucifix. I wonder what ever happened to that thing. It wasn't big, but it dripped fake jewels—ruby, amethyst, and amber—reminded me of the absurdity of everything.

By Christmas night, the storm had said its piece, and for seven days nothing fell from the sky. Still, the snow and ice refused to melt. The passes remained closed. Streets were left unplowed. We waited, frozen.

Lupe listened to her conch shell and watched the moon out the window.

Pia shook her snow globe, and Magdelena bleached her hair.

Barbaro read to me from his new book about a clown not contented just to make people laugh but who dreamed of imparting a lasting joy. "I am this clown," Barbaro said. "I wish to rejuvenate battered souls."

Tony plucked his bass, and Paula seemed to know just how to sing Manny to sleep.

At least we weren't in Baltimore anymore.

Some nights in that motel, just as I was about to fall asleep, I had the most brilliant ideas—bright spheres of weightless jade full of insights you wouldn't believe. I kept a pen and notebook under my pillow, hoping, just once, to catch even a glimmer of that late-night lucidity, but even with the waking energy it took to sit up, to turn on the fake porcelain lamp, to reach for the pen, the revelation had already floated away like an early-morning dream.

I wrote only: *Dazzling.*

On the third day of the new year, when the sun finally seared us a path out of there, I don't think there was even so much as a discussion about whether or not Paula would take the stage. Motel room lullabies just morphed into interstate rehearsals, and interstate rehearsals morphed into the obvious: We had a seventh player.

Paula knew all about her namesake—the legendary saint with the beard, fourteenth-century Spanish gal who'd been pursued by every man in town until one day, at her wit's end dealing with an overardent suitor, she fled into the local Catholic church and embraced the crucifix, begged her Savior to deliver her from the stalker. Immediately, a beard grew on her face, effectively deterring all present and future men.

"I think beards are sexy," Magdelena protested when she heard the story. "Especially on girls."

"What do you think of the whole Catholic theme?" Tony wanted to know.

Paula just laughed. "I'm iron tracks," she said, "nailed to unforgiving earth."

And so it was that when we finally rolled into St. Louis for our show at the Hi Pointe Café, iron tracks took her place in the dark, hands clasped in front of her, and as the makeshift spotlight rose, she began to sing.

What I wouldn't give now to rewind to that uncomplicated night.

Mary Magdalen

(IF YOU NEED FORGIVENESS)

A.K.A. The sinner
FEAST DAY: July 22
SYMBOLS: a mirror, a skull, a scarlet egg

There exists no evidence, scriptural or otherwise, that Mary
Magdalen was a whore. The rumors of prostitution were written into Latin tradition some half a millennium after the crucifixion. How'd they do it? And why? Simple. The church took it
upon itself to merge the Gospel stories of Mary Magdalen,
Mary of Bethany, and an unnamed woman sinner who washed
Jesus's feet with her tears, dried them with her long hair, then
anointed them with expensive perfume oil from the Himalayas.
Reading into the text that the unnamed sinner was a prosti-
tute (because how else could a girl afford that kind of perfume?) and then inventing the possibility that the three women
were one, the church got themselves a high-priced hooker who
fell for the Savior, a redeemed whore, a model of repentance
weeping guilty-sorry for all female knowledge and sin.

See, the church was on a real antisex kick at the
time—*what else is new?*—and they needed an example of
female sexuality reined in. That's Pope Gregory the Great for
you. Even the Vatican has since admitted—albeit in the liturgi-
cal equivalent of fine print—that it was all nonsense and con-
jecture. A smear campaign, really.

Gnostic Gospels, written at the same time as the New
Testament but not chosen for inclusion, place Mary Magdalen

more constantly at Christ's side—the thirteenth disciple, Our Savior's partner and companion, apostle of the apostles, a forceful preacher competing with the guys for leadership in the early church. The New Testament, well edited to leave out anything that might undermine male dominance and church power, mentions only Mary Magdalen's role in the crucifixion and its aftermath.

According to John, three Marys—Jesus's mother, aunt, and Magdalen—stood by the execution cross like the old Pagan triple goddess.

On Sunday, Mary Magdalen went to the tomb where she'd seen Joseph of Arimathea place the Lord's body. Finding the stone rolled away and the body gone, she ran to find Peter and another disciple to tell them what had happened. The two returned with her, saw the burial linen inside the otherwise empty tomb, but then the men went home to mourn in their own ways. Mary Magdalen wept alone. When two angels appeared and asked her why she was crying, she said, "Someone has taken my Lord's body and I do not know where." Turning, she saw another man who asked her why she wept. Thinking he might be a gardener, she asked him if he'd seen where they'd taken the body.

The man opened his vast compassionate heart, only had to say a single word: "Mary."

She didn't flinch. She knew she was in her Lord's presence. She stood, inheritor of the light, witness and herald of the new life.

"Do not cling to me," he said, "for I am not yet ascended to the Father."

Those seeking inner vision and the contemplative life light a candle for Mary Magdalen and whisper, "So that I may not waver at the sight of the divine."

To honor her, learn to express your grief as well as your joy. Watch the sunrise or sunset and say out loud, "I am fully and radiantly myself, immune to slander. I offer my unique gift to the world." Stay open to inner vision and refrain from judgment. That woman you're calling a whore might just be the Lord's favorite apostle, and that gardener you hope to underpay might be God himself.

Once, when it was just me and Magdelena driving the second hatchback from Madison to Minneapolis, she insisted that we take a detour to stop at the World's Largest Replica Cheese. She'd always had a soft place in her heart, she said, for the story of the World's Largest Cheese—a seventeen-ton cheddar displayed for two consecutive years at the New York World's Fair. She'd seen it once, the real cheese, when it toured America in the glass-sided Cheesemobile, and she'd always regretted having no memory of the event. She was only a baby, taken on her mother's hip to see the grand result of the combined efforts of the Wisconsin Cheese Foundation and sixteen thousand cows. She would have preferred to stop and see the real cheese, of course, but, alas, the Wisconsin Dairymen had eaten the thing.

At least they had the heart to replace it with a replica.

We cut off the main route, headed into Neillsville. And there next to the Wisconsin Pavilion—now a radio station—we visited not one but two world's largest things: the replica cheese and Chatty Belle, the world's largest talking cow. The sixteen-foot fiberglass Holstein greeted us when we dropped a quarter into her voice box, saying, "Hi, so nice to see you." And, "A cow my size would produce over two hundred seventy pounds of milk a day."

A semitrailer housed the giant orange replica cheese. *What was it made of?* I thought Styrofoam, Magdelena guessed plywood.

I'm not sure why this is what I think of as I creep into Magdelena's dressing room now, my High Sierra wildflowers drooping in their mason jar, a paltry offering. Not even close to the world's largest anything.

She sits in front of the mirror, applying Great Lash mascara.

I thought I'd be able to tell, as soon as I saw Magdelena, whether Barbaro's story was true or tall. Instead, I can't seem to remember why it mattered so much. I hate it when that happens—when something that seemed so important just a few days or hours earlier suddenly loses its meaning. Her cigarette teeters at the edge of her dressing table. She circles her eyes with black liner. I try to focus, remind myself why it matters—the identity of my betrayer—but I can't seem to manage even a humble indignation. Who is Magdelena, after all, but a girl who never meant to turn thirty? I have to admit—even if it's only in fine print—that I've never known Magdelena to betray anyone at all.

When she sees me in the mirror, she sets down her kohl stick, watches me in silence like maybe she's imagined, too, that she'd be able to tell something when she saw me, but it's as if both our eyes are just white stones. Two people who've traveled together for seven years but still don't know the first thing about one another. Finally she fractures the quiet with a sigh. "I probably would have thought the same thing, Frankka."

I take a deep breath. From my back pocket, I produce Magdelena's old red silk camisole. I washed it in a sink at the bus station in Stockton, but it doesn't look nearly as precious as it did the night I stole it—that shimmering promise of sexy-cool. "I took this."

She doesn't seem surprised, says only, "Thanks," as I place it on her dressing table.

I hold out the flowers, shrug stupidly. "I brought these for you and Pia."

Now Pia stands filling the doorway, as if magnetically drawn to the mention of her name. She smiles, sad-hurt, and I know all the greed in this room is my own. Ever since that night in our student house in Santa Cruz when Tony told me I had star talent without the necessary ego, I'd dreamed of outshining them all. Blanketed vanity.

"So the hypochondriac's come down from the mountain," Pia says. That's the way she talks when she doesn't want to get hurt by anyone anymore. Just trying to be an oak.

I place the flowers on the table, not quite sure what to say next. I hadn't rehearsed anything, had imagined some lengthy processing session, but what's there to process, really? "I didn't—" I start to say, but Pia just holds up her large hand.

The silence tastes like shattered rocks. I want to turn everything into gravel.

"Big venue," I finally say.

Pia nods, looks me up and down. "I certainly hope you're not planning on performing in that outfit."

My dried mud jeans and sweaty *Sesame Street* T-shirt. I clutch my plastic bag of new clothes. "No," I promise. "Wouldn't dream of it."

Barbaro's red and white canvas backpack sits in the corner, propped against a black wall. I take the smiling newspaper clown from my other pocket, smooth it out, and place it on top of his bag.

Magdelena winks at me, knocks back her shot of brandy.

"Break a leg," Pia says.

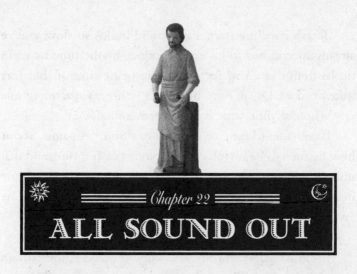

Chapter 22

ALL SOUND OUT

Close your eyes.

The audience waits in a pool of darkness, seated and hushed, waiting for miracles.

I can feel my heart pounding even in my veins. Sometimes a moment can last so long. Volcanic mountains and hundred-mile views. A starless homeless night. Moonlight shining in limestone caves. A miraculous heart preserved in a stone cathedral.

Madre Pia's great bellowing voice explodes into the black: "In the beginning God created the heavens and the earth. And the earth was without form, and void. And darkness was upon the face of the deep. And the spirit moved across the face of the waters. And God said, *Let there be light!*"

A billow of flame bursts from stage left.

Madre lifts her hands and the lights rise, illuminating shy Paula the Bearded as she begins to sing like some lost shorebird in the burnt night.

Tony's bass line starts so low and builds so slow, you've already succumbed to his craving trance by the time he picks up his tenor sax. You recognize the beginning of that jazz suite from a CD you once heard in a stranger's apartment in a city whose skyline you no longer remember.

Backstage, Manny tells me about Snuffleupagus, about how he used to be invisible to everyone but Big Bird, and that nobody believed he even existed. "But he was real!" Manny insists, stretching out his arms. As I hand him off to Paula, he says, "I wanna build a LEGO castle!"

New day, new state, same show.

I join Magdelena, Tony, and Lupe onstage as the curtain rises deliciously familiar on this small circle of friends. We sing and clown, make music and dance, drink and laugh like nothing's ever been fucked up between us, and I imagine my fellow travelers aren't just performing. They love me still, don't they? Like *famiglia*.

Barbaro waits in the shadows, watching, but each time he starts to approach, we push him away. Stranger. Outsider. Betrayer. Asshole or liar or worse. Repentant sinner.

Focus on the performance, Frankka.

Barbaro rustles though his bag for his carnival mask, tries to get our attention, but we refuse to be taken in by his antics.

Tony plays a few notes on his saxophone before he launches into his old narcotic lullaby.

We sway sleepy as the lights dim. All quiet now.

I can see silhouettes in the audience.

Then a racket from stage right. Madre's heavy footfalls. She appears in black, her face wrinkled-wounded. She grabs me. I let her drag my limp body, content to be a victim to her merciful love.

Barbaro, the only witness to my arrest, hastens to wake the others. He points, panicked, as the curtain falls.

I take my place center stage now. Curtain up, and I extend my arms, crosslike.

Bass line like a heartbeat, and the friends come rushing with Barbaro, too late.

The lights are a blinding wall of white heat. I close my eyes and force my appetite up from my belly and into my head. I will my mind empty of everything but the hunger, press it out through my shoulders, though my muscles and veins. I envision the blood traveling down my arms like a lava flow. My palms feel hot. I tremble, just a little, but when I open my eyes to glance at my hands, no blood flows. I concentrate on my hunger, on the sheer hollowness of my belly, on my arms and hands, but the emptiness won't hold. Three fish in a bucket.

Go away, fish. No thoughts now. My silver rainbow trout.

Push them out of your mind, Frankka.

I think of my grandmother, weeping in her golden armchair. "Nana," I whisper faintly.

From the hush of the audience, a sudden heckle. "She's a fraud!"

I open my eyes, but there's no one there. Just the glare of bright lights.

"Nothing's happening!" someone yells.

A mumbling rustle of bodies in the dark.

Then a sound, sharp and abrupt—*bpooom.*

An unbridled shriek.

The smell of gunfire.

My field of vision, a panning blurred disorientation of lights.

Shouts and footfalls in the aisles. *Bpooom.*

Magdelena leaps from nowhere, tackles me to the stage.

Just as I hit my head, a child's screech. "Butt aaassssss!" And another shot echoes through the theater. My foot explodes.

A siren scream. "Emaaanuel!"

All sound out. The world fades to black.

A beating of wings, a searing pain. The skull bird bursts forth and flies, its white wings like a dream of angels.

Lights, hands, movement, pain, sirens, wind, red. *Hail Mary full of grace, the Lord is with you.* Movement, lights, cloth, eyes, hands, chill. *Blessed art thou among women and blessed is the fruit of thy womb.* Lights, questions, hands, pain, movement, needles. *Holy Mary, Mother of God, pray for us sinners now and at the hour of our death.*

Chapter 23

DEMEROL

He appears in a dawny coral glow, wears a halo of moonlight.

Hush.

"Who are you?"

He doesn't answer, holds out his hand, scarred at the wrist, offers me something crimson and pulsing.

I try to focus on his dark legacy.

In his other hand, a sharp paring knife glints in the strange glow. Gently, he takes the knife to my chest. The blade is cold as he cuts me open and places his gift inside me, saying, "Dearest daughter, as I took your heart away, now, you see, I am giving you mine."

"In self-knowledge," Catherine of Siena wrote, "you will humble yourself, seeing that, in yourself, you do not even exist."

He's gone, just like that. Only the coral glow remains.

I can hear the heart beat faintly, like a faraway train.

I wake woozy to a world of white: white sheets, white walls, white ceiling, white floors, white curtains opening to white skies, white uniformed seraphs in white masks shuffling under white lights. They smell of lilies. It's like we're already in heaven but for the other smell. Surely heaven doesn't smell of lemon disinfectant.

I search my dream mind for the man haloed in silvery light. "Come back," I whisper, my hands and feet seared in a dull and wanting pain.

He presses his hand to my chest, instantly healing the scar left by the paring knife.

My eyelids are heavy, but I manage to lift them. My foot tended and wrapped, heavy, too. I can feel something around my head, reach to touch the bandage.

Barbaro stands at my bedside. "They have said you must not go," he tells me. "But in fact we must go."

"Go where?" Throat parched, whole body heavy, head pulsing, chest raw. "Did I get shot in the head?"

"No," Barbaro assures me. "You have been shot in the foot. You hit your head on a stage platform." His face blurs and he's standing in a courtyard in the snow, white flakes in his dark hair, blowing a grand plume of fire. My strange prehistoric bird of an angel.

I close my eyes and I'm climbing a ladder. I'm looking for my haloed man, but when I reach the final rung, there's only the bright Easter image from my grandmother's living room. White cloaked and well fed, Our Savior stands perfectly still, arms outstretched, glowing like the sun behind him, palms still bleeding from his Good Friday ordeal. I say, "I want the real you, not my personal mythology."

But he doesn't answer. It's Barbaro's voice I hear. "I have for you a wheelchair."

I fall backward from my ladder, fall for a long time. Wispy clouds, sky the color of bubblegum ice cream. I don't need a wheelchair. Heavy limbed, foot smoldering like a black-orange coal, but crutches would certainly do. "No," I say out loud, but even as I say it, I let Barbaro help me into the chair. "Where are we?"

I am wheeled under fluorescent lights, brought to a pause in a windowless purgatory of empty chairs and humming coffee machines. A muted television mounted near the ceiling.

"Are you ready to be awake?" Barbaro asks.

"Ready?"

He lifts the morning paper from a low table, points to a twisted face that looks like it's made of clay: an unfinished bust in some sculptor's studio. A body dragged by rough hands, a bold headline:

GOD TOLD ME TO KILL HER

"There are many pigs in this hospital," Barbaro says. "You will have to speak."

Oh, make them blind to me.

I take the newspaper from Barbaro, try to read the tangled mess of words that confirm the dense-world obvious: *Frances Catherine, the stigmatic performance artist . . .* That clean bullet was meant for my heart.

Barbaro holds a Styrofoam cup of milky coffee in front of me. "Drink this," he says.

Will it make me bigger or smaller? Will it seal my scars?

"Do not be terrified," Barbaro says.

★   ★   ★

Down seven long white hallways, I sip the coffee, careful not to spill it as Barbaro pushes me around corners, faster and faster.

Slow down is what I'm thinking, but a new panic rises in my gut as we approach our fellow travelers. They stand like spectators, looking through a sea of glass mingled with fire and into a white room.

On the other side, Manny lies silent, only his sweet bronze face visible from under white sheets. The shock of black hair. He could be sleeping, dreaming in some nameless motel room at the edge of some nameless highway, but wires and tubes connect his small body to an IV drip and computerized monitors: Beep, beep, beep. That mechanical bird, communicating without words. Beep, beep, beep.

Lupe kneels at her son's bedside.

A uniformed cop stands sturdy at the door.

We are to keep our distance.

"He has survived the surgery," Barbaro explains. "However, his condition remains critical. He is so small. He has entered a coma."

The bullet meant for my heart. My guilt tastes like tar.

My fellow travelers stand, gargling their own thick self-hatred. Tony lured mother and child from the safe womb of their adobe in the desert, did he not? Promised to keep them safe on the road. Barbaro opened his big trusting mouth to high-heeled Judy when she pretended to be friend and confidant. Paula failed to build the LEGO castle Manny wanted. "Let's go see the show," she pleaded with him. "It might be the last time. I'll let you sit front and center." Pia heard the first shot, but she didn't register it, so focused was she on her mystical levitation. Magdelena tackled me to safety. Surely if I'd caught the first bullet, the shooter would have relented, satisfied.

And Lupe, crouched next to her baby now, head bent and shaking. Lupe, who had the audacity to bring a bright and defenseless new soul into this mean and knotted world. All the sins of humanity pile on her trembling shoulders.

"Frances Catherine?"

I turn, and there's a tall black cop standing over me. His badge gleams like armor under the lights. "If we could talk to you for a few minutes?"

I know his question isn't a question so much as a demand. I glance up at Barbaro, hoping for a cue, but he just nods and shrugs, tears pooling in his chocolate eyes. I could easily wheel myself, but Barbaro rushes to push me down the white linoleum-tiled hallway, following the cop. Penance, or something like it.

In the waiting room, a pudgy white guy who looks more like a gangster than a cop asks me the questions. The tall one stands by like a guard, arms folded. "Did you see the person who shot you, Frances?"

"No." Those hot and blinding lights that eradicate the audience. "I was onstage."

"Do you know anyone who would want to harm you, Frances?"

"No one in particular," I tell him. My head hurts.

"I understand that you never talked to the investigator from the Sacramento Police Department after the pipe bomb was found under your car, Frances?"

I hate those people who tack your name on the end of every sentence. "No," I say. "No one contacted me."

"Is there anyone you owe money to, anything like that? Old vendettas, Frances?"

Money? Old vendettas? I can't tell if his questions are ridiculous or if it's me who's cloudy headed. "It's just—I'm assuming it's just they don't like my show." As soon as I've said it I realize it sounds just as preposterous as anything he could come up with. "I don't even know that many people," I add dumbly.

The tall cop shakes his head, doesn't say anything.

The white cop narrows his eyes. "Someone would have to dislike your show an awful lot to try to kill you in two separate cities, don't you think, Frances?"

It seems strange that he's trying to find something particularly off about a guy with a gun. Like there are certain paths of logic that would make it okay to try and kill someone in two separate cities—normal, in fact. "Was it the same person?"

"Do *you* think it was the same person, Frances?"

"How would I know?" If my body wasn't so heavy in my chair, I might start getting defensive. It's like he thinks I know something. It's like he knows this is all my fault.

"Where were you the night they found the bomb under your car, Frances?"

I clear my throat. *Where was I?* "Lying low." I regret the words as soon as I've said them, but I don't know how much these guys already know and I don't want to tell them about the tunnel or the old minister, about the terror on TV or the phone call. "I didn't hear about the bomb until I saw it in the paper," I lie, just praying it was in the paper at all.

"And when you did hear about it, you didn't think it would be a good idea to contact the Sacramento Police Department, Frances?"

"I haven't had a chance," I say honestly, but of course it sounds like a lie.

"Why haven't you claimed your car, Frances?"

"It's not really my car," I admit. "I was just driving it that day . . . I—"

"Do you know this man, Frances?" the cop shoves a picture in my lap. It's the man from the newspaper, but this one's a mug shot. A round-faced scowl. That strange countenance made of clay. I imagine rubbing away the layers to reveal his child-face. *Why would God tell a guy like that to kill me?* Maybe God really is some kind of an asshole, waking people up in the middle of the night and commanding them to commit murder.

"I've never seen him before in my life. Or, well, I saw him in the paper this morning."

"And I suppose you don't know whose car is sitting unclaimed in Sacramento, Frances?"

I didn't know the car was left. The little red hatchback with New Mexico plates and stolen tags because Lupe didn't want to go back through Albuquerque even to renew the registration. My duffel in the trunk. I say, "Am I in trouble?" You never know when they'll come for you, and here I am wearing nothing but a white hospital gown.

"Why would you be in trouble, Frances? You're the *vic*-tim, right, Frances?" He says the word *victim* with all this venom on the *vic,* spitting it out, leaving the second syllable to a whisper.

I say, "I really don't know what happened, officer. There was a big crowd in Sacramento and I got scared. I went camping for a couple of days to clear my head. Then I came back to meet my troupe here in Los Angeles. We did the show at the Hermosa Beach Playhouse and somebody shot Manny."

"Somebody shot you, too, Frances."

Mea culpa, I want to tell him. *Sinner, impure, forgive me.* But a police questioning is no place for confessions.

Paula stands at my side now. She says, "Frances Catherine is still recovering from surgery. If you have any more questions, she'll be happy to answer them when our lawyer arrives."

Who knew Paula would turn out to be such a tactician? Silent when folks are partying, but always there to save our sorry asses when things get sticky.

I wonder what time it is. No windows here.

═══ ✝ ═══

I spent all night in a hospital waiting room once before. I lay on my babysitter's lap, but I didn't sleep. I don't even remember her name—my babysitter's. She wore little unicorn decals on her long, pale pink fingernails. Just a woman. Probably a teenager. *Who knows?* Maybe I've invented the whole memory-scene. She smelled of peach nectar.

I later learned that my father was already dead when we got to the hospital, my mother clinging to life in a white bed in a white room, attached to a lifeless machine. But my babysitter couldn't have known those things or she wouldn't have packed me into her little purple Honda and perked, "Change of plans! Gotta go meet your parents at the hospital. They crashed the car!"

I understood my babysitter's words that night to mean that I wouldn't see the car again, or that I would see it and it would be smashed and mangled like cars on TV. Nothing more grave. I wondered if we could still get my Winnie the Pooh doll out of the back seat. *Change of plans.* My parents had promised not to be gone long, and it had been a long time. Still, what did time mean to me then? It *seemed* like it had been a long time. I waited. No windows, but surely morning was breaking when the doctor finally emerged in her white uniform, saying only, "I'm sorry."

My babysitter rose to meet her.

They spoke in hushed tones, the tones grown-ups speak in when they're going to give you a present. It occurred to me that the woman in white was hiding my parents in some unseen room.

Calls were made, presumably.

I waited on the puffy vinyl bench alone, wiggling my toes in my footed green pajamas.

When my babysitter finally came back, she had tears in her eyes and no present. "I'm sorry, baby," is all she said. She scooped me up in those teenage arms that seemed so big to me. "We shouldn't have come here." Her hair was long and dark and soft like my mother's.

Then the endless tired winding sunrise drive up Highway 1 from Santa Cruz in that little purple Honda. I whined, "I don't *wanna* go see my Nana." The old woman had always petrified me, the mass of black polyester and cotton. How could I have understood that she'd become my closest blood relation on this blue planet?

"I want my *moooom*," I insisted.

"I'm so sorry." That's all my babysitter would say.

From the car window, I watched the ocean.

Chapter 24
A MONK IN THE SKY

In the white bathroom, I have to hang onto railings and hop for the toilet. Sharpie graffiti on the wall tells me: *God is dead —Nietzsche.* And in another handwriting: *Nietzsche is dead —God.*

In front of the mirror, I unwrap the bandage from my head, admire the plum welt just above my right eyebrow. I tie my hair into a quick knot.

Back out in the waiting room, Tony cries silent under a muted television.

I wheel myself over next to him. "Hey—"

He doesn't look up. He talks into his own hands. "To live is to cause suffering."

"This isn't your fault," I try, even though, in a way, I know it is.

"There are so many ways to mess everything up and so few ways to make things right. Do you know what I'm talking about, Frankka?"

This time I do. I know exactly what he's talking about.

He says, "You were right to leave the show in Sacramento. We all should have left. We should have run away—up into the mountains or out into the desert—anywhere. Lupe didn't want to continue, but the rest of us kept saying, 'The show must go on,' like we're a bunch of stubborn little kids reciting some stupid theater slogan. Lupe didn't want to file the claim to get the car back, either, so we figured we'd humor her with that one, go along with it, and then maybe she'd drop her superstitious nonsense about bad luck and omens and canceling shows we'd already booked. 'We're in danger,' that's what she kept saying. 'We're in danger.' But we ignored her like elevator music. I thought she was PMSing or something. I said, 'Come on, Lupe, you'll probably get your period tomorrow and this'll all seem like a bad dream. We've dealt with protesters before. You've never tripped. The show must go on.' "

I wrap my fingers around Tony's arm. "You couldn't have known this would happen."

He cries into his hands. "*She* knew."

An old man paces in the waiting room. Other terrors are unfolding here in other white rooms.

Paula enters with the slim stranger from the Hermosa Beach Playhouse, and they take the two empty seats next to Tony.

The stranger smiles at me. "I'm a friend of Paula's."

I nod.

Tony says, "Manny's going to die."

"Who shall we pray to?" Barbaro wants to know. He holds out a pair of crutches, looks at me like I'm going to have an answer.

"I don't know."

He touches my forehead as I stand. "Of course you know," he says. "You are Saint Cat."

As if it were so simple. *The real thing pretending to be a fraud.* Maybe he sees through me. Or maybe he's just hoping because what we need right now is a saint.

"He's going to die," Tony says again.

"Shut up," Paula snaps. "Haven't you ever heard of *positive thinking?*"

Barbaro looks up at me, and I wish I had some magic trick to make all this suffering go away. "We should pray," he insists.

In the white hallway outside Manny's room, I lean on my crutches. The seven of us join hands in a semicircle. We watch through that thick glass. Beep, beep, beep.

Everyone's looking at me like I'm the one in charge here, so I guess I am. "I'll tell you a story."

Padre Pio

(IF YOU NEED A MIRACLE HEALING)

A.K.A. Pio of Pietrelcina
FEAST DAY: September 23
SYMBOLS: a rosary, fiery skies

In a mountain town in southern Italy near the place the Black Madonna of the Poor once appeared in an oak tree, Francesco Forgione was born to a poor farming family in 1887. The whole area was known for its healers, but also for its poverty. After years of crop failures, many of the town's men went to America looking for steady wages.

A daddy's boy, Francesco was heartbroken when his own father left home to work on the Erie Railroad. Forlorn, the seven-year-old told his mother he wanted to become a monk. Maybe he could replace his father with The Father. But Orazio Forgione wasn't off working in America so his kids could be illiterate like he was. Francesco could be a monk, fair enough—he could even be a priest—but first he'd be educated. Francesco stayed in school, but he was a quirky little thing. Never quite fit in. He prayed like a maniac, secretly went without food or drink for days on end. He was barely nine years old when his mom discovered that he'd been sleeping on the floor with a stone for a pillow. The kids at school called him "macaroni without salt"—he couldn't run, couldn't jump, couldn't climb trees. *What was he good for?* "No one knows what will become of Francesco," the town priest said.

Macaroni without salt, maybe, but Francesco soon discovered his healing powers. As a young teenager, he received a gift of some chestnuts from a neighbor woman, returned the cloth bag they came in. The woman sensed something magical about the boy, so she saved the bag. When a barn explosion left her seriously injured, she placed the bag on her wound, and, miraculously, she was healed.

When Francesco finally left home to follow his dreams of Capuchin monkhood, he took the name Pio, but he was put out of one monastery and then another for refusing to eat. When he got back home, he was delighted to see his family and friends—and they him—but it wasn't long before they noticed that something was wrong. Night after night when Pio retired to his room, neighbors heard screams and the sound of solid bodies hitting the floor. The first time it happened, his mother rushed to his room, flung the door open. Books and inkwells had been thrown around the room, bed blankets scattered, chairs upside down. Pio stood in the chaos, silent. *Nutcase or holy man?*

Eventually he moved into the monastery at San Giovanni Rotundo, not far from his hometown. Maybe he had weird eating habits and noisy nighttime antics, but there was something special about Padre Pio. With his powers of clairvoyance, he could locate missing soldiers, and with the touch of his hand, hunchbacks stood upright.

His fame as a healer was already spreading across Italy when, at the age of thirty-one, he experienced a transverberation. He'd been hearing a young boy's confession when an angel appeared in his mind's eye. The angel held a long steel blade that spewed flames. Suddenly, and with the force of some mad warrior, the angel hurled the blade into his soul. Padre Pio thought he'd die of the pain, thought that surely some internal organ had ruptured. He told the confessing boy to leave, that he felt too ill to continue. All night he languished in agony. A month and a half later, as the priest knelt in front of a large crucifix, he swooned, suddenly tired. And the vision appeared again. Blood dripped from the angel's hands, feet, and side. When he came to, Padre Pio had received the stigmata—all five wounds of Christ. He was put under medical observation immediately—only doctors were allowed to seal and unseal his bandages—but the doctors couldn't stop the bleeding, and they could find no natural cause.

News of the miracle-making modern priest with the stigmata brought pilgrims from all over the world, turning San Giovanni Rotundo into a veritable Graceland, but within the church, controversy bloomed. Folks accused Padre Pio of stabbing himself to make his palms and feet bleed. They called him hysterical, called him a fraud, called him worse. In an attempt to quiet the whole thing down, the church silenced the bleeding priest in 1923, forbidding him to write letters or give sermons. He obliged, but church authorities were too late. Padre Pio was a rock star. The faithful and the curious still flocked to southern Italy to confess their sins. And the church finally relented.

Padre Pio performed miraculous healings, if not in person then via bilocation—quicker and cheaper than train travel. "I feel all your troubles as if they were my own," he said. He hardly ever left San Giovanni Rotundo, but he was seen all over the world—from Hawaii to St. Peter's, where he made an unexpected appearance at the canonization of the Little Flower Thérèse of Lisieux.

Boyishly devoted to his guardian angel, old "macaroni without salt" reminded his followers that if he didn't pick up their prayer-calls himself, they could always leave a message with his angel. "I sleep with a smile of sweet beatitude on my lips," he said. "And a perfectly tranquil countenance, waiting for the little companion of my childhood to come to waken me, so that we may sing together the morning praises."

That angel arrived every morning long before sunrise—2:30 A.M., and the two of them already up and praying, preparing for mass and hearing confessions. Padre Pio's full workday lasted nineteen hours, but he subsisted on just a few hundred calories a day: some boiled vegetables and a half glass of beer at noontime. All the while, his five wounds oozed a blood that smelled of roses.

Military records from World War II confirm that on many occasions, when Allied forces attempted to bomb San Giovanni Rotundo, a monk was seen in the sky, directing the planes to turn around.

Imagine the look on those commanding officers' faces when their pilots returned to base, bombs still on board, explaining, "Sir, yes, sir, but see there was this monk in the clouds . . ."

That monk was Padre Pio.

In 1968, the old priest finally surrendered to Sister Death. He performs his miracles from heaven now. A devotee tells the story about when her kids were young and she'd gathered them to pray. She lit the candles, asked Padre Pio to join the family. When they were finished, she put Our Lady's statue away, and one of the little ones asked, "Mom, who was that old man in the brown robe saying the rosary with us?"

That old man was Padre Pio.

We honor him by imagining wings on our feet. We protect what we love. We wear yellow and walk at dawn or dusk, calling out to the horizon, "I vow that every gift I am given, I will share with the world." We wink at our guardian angels, saying, "I know we haven't talked much since we were kids, but I'm willing to be childish if it means you'll always be with me."

"Close your eyes." We stand silent in our own darkness, facing Manny on the other side. A gentle gust of wind seems to push us from behind and we're carried forward. "Do not waver," I whisper, and with a sudden gale force like the wind off an open lake, we're swept through the glass. We stand, encircling mother and child, praying silent crazy desperate to the old man in the brown robe to bilocate from heaven and give us a miracle we can sink our guilty teeth into. "Beloved Padre Pio, today we come to add our prayer to the thousands of prayers offered to you every day by those who love and venerate you. They ask for cures and healings, earthly and spiritual blessings, peace for body and mind. Because of your friendship with the Lord, he heals those you ask to be healed and forgives those you forgive. Beloved and humble . . ." I imagine Padre Pio in his brown cape, swooping down from the sky like a comic book superhero, his guardian angel at his back, but Padre Pio isn't the one who shows up.

"How'd *she* get past the cop?" Paula whispers.

I look up as the heavy body moves through us and toward the white-sheeted bed. "Nana?"

She waves in my direction, but she's focused on the baby. "He's in a loneliness awash with light," she says. "There's no one to meet him yet." She kneels down next to Lupe. "Pray," she commands.

I lean on my crutches at the foot of the bed. "Pray, but how?" And all at once out of my thick blue grief it occurs to me that—messed up as I am, scarred and bandaged, sorry and lost—there exists some small excess of grace that dances like dust particles just above my head. I concentrate on Manny's figure under the sheets, envision my particles gathering above my head and pouring from me and into him.

The heart monitor: beep, beep, beep.

A nurse appears in white. "There's too many people in here!" But then she falls silent. "Oh, my God."

What does she see?

I concentrate on my grace particles. I'd expected to force them all to Manny in an instant, but somehow they just keep flowing, multiplying as they stream from my head to his core.

Pia rises slowly over the bed, and Paula begins to sing her low, sweet hymn.

A rustling from somewhere.

Beep, beep, beep.

"Pray," my grandmother orders us, a vein of worry cutting across her forehead. "There's someone coming to meet him now."

Manny lies cold and still as a museum installation.

The nurse watches, frozen, as the grace particles all stream from our crowns and into the baby.

A knock at the door, three quick raps, but I ignore it, will the sound away, will Sister Death far from this white room.

Wait.

Another sound, but this one like a crystal glass being struck by a metal rod, like a memory of water.

Manny's body radiates through the sheets and the chemical lemon air, burning through our guilt like acid. He doesn't open his eyes, but there's a quick movement behind his lids, like he's dreaming for real.

"Emanuel?" Lupe whispers.

Pia rises higher as Paula's song wings to an end.

"Big Bird?" Manny whispers.

My grandmother looks up, her face glowing unwrinkled under the lights. "No," she says. "He isn't coming yet."

"Where'd Big Bird go?" That's all the baby wants to know when he opens his heavy lids.

"Another time," my grandmother whispers, touching his forehead lightly with her finger. "Another time, my child."

Chapter 25
THE CLAY FACE

In the windowless room, the cops wait for Lupe, eager with their damn photo.

"Just leave her alone—" I say. But of course they will not.

When she finally emerges, she hasn't eaten or slept for two nights. She holds Tony's arm to steady her walk.

"Lupe?"

Like they have any right to call her by her first name.

"We know this is a difficult time for you."

Disoriented, Lupe thanks them. She's still wearing her blue costume from the show.

The gangster cop thrusts the mug shot in her face. "Do you know this man, Lupe?"

She stares at the face, silent.

"Have you ever seen this man before, Lupe?"

Dark eyes, thin lips.

Tony and I stand on either side of her, waiting for her denial, but she's quiet.

"Lupe?"

It's like the cops know something.

Lupe nods slowly.

"Did you see this man in Sacramento, Lupe?"

The tall one leans in. "Or maybe you saw him when you stole his *car*?"

"*Shh,*" his partner whispers, like maybe they're going to get something out of this stunned mother after all.

Lupe's expression doesn't change. She says, "That's my husband."

Chapter 26

WHAT YOU WOULD HAVE ME DO

Keep traveling? Stay in Los Angeles to help Lupe and Tony through Manny's recovery? Get rich? Become famous? Settle down and learn to be a good neighbor? Heal the sick? Train myself to bilocate? Give butter away? Find love and offer my heart without expectation? Found monasteries? Deny the body? Multiply loaves? Surrender to Your mysterious will? Sit cross-legged in a cave until I achieve enlightenment? If I only knew the central challenge of my life, I could do it—I know I could. I could accomplish anything. But what is it? Why am I here? *I'll pour myself into your work, God, just tell me what you would have me do.*

★ ★ ★

The proposal comes at me so pure and surreal, I never would have dared to dream it up. It unfolds like an epic rambling dream I just wake understanding and all the more so because it seems like ages since I've had the courage to even pray for anything *right*. I've always been careful not to hope too big for fear of offending God with my ambition or, worse, my greed. Or maybe my trepidation has more to do with that nagging fear of disappointment, but—no—I prefer to think of it as humility in the face of the divine. I'm faithful in my way. I do the best I can.

Barbaro kneels on the shag-carpeted floor of our Redondo Beach motel room. "I have for you a proposition."

I smile, embarrassed, still groggy from my drugs and just a little bit tipsy now from a single glass of wine. "Are you going to ask me to marry you?" I laugh.

Barbaro makes an awkward back-and-forth gesture with his head. "Not exactly, no." He clears his throat. "If you agree to my proposal, please remember this entire scene. We will describe it again and again to many pigs as a tremendous and commencing moment."

I bite my lip. *What's he talking about?* The taste of cheap Chianti on my tongue, the smell of kung pao shrimp and moo-shu vegetables in the red and white takeout boxes on the round wooden table. The heavy brown curtains and beds with matching polyester spreads. The large TV, the brown minifridge, the microwave oven. The Mr. Perks coffeemaker and tub of dry coffee. The packets of sugar and creamer. The nightstand with the Goodwill brown lamp and the copy of Gideon's Bible. The phone book and guest services binder that amounts to a few Chinese food ads. My foot bandaged.

The plum of a lump on my forehead, still pulsing achy. I'm wearing the brown wool sweater Dorothy gave me for my predawn journey down from the mountains as Barbaro kneels in the glittering candlelight. *This whole scene.*

Barbaro reaches into the pocket of his black hoodie, fumbles around before producing—*what is it?*—a small platinum ring with three sparkling stones. His hand shakes a little as he holds it up in the candlelight.

"Are those diamonds, Barbaro?"

"No," he blushes. "Cubic zirconia." He readjusts his position on the floor in front of me. "Frankka," he says, "with this ring, I am asking for your hand in a mythical marriage."

His words plume through the air toward me like fire, but I'm mystified. "I don't get it."

Barbaro swallows, nervous. He holds up the ring, runs his free hand though his short hair. He says, "I am proposing to give you this ring, Frankka, for drama."

I can hear waves crashing somewhere. I wonder how near we are to the ocean. "For drama?"

"Yes," Barbaro says. "While at the hospital, I received papers from the Department of Homeland Security. I have been given thirty days to depart from this country or appear before a judge. I have decided that I would prefer to return to Italia, to the Free University in Umbria whose motto is 'Life is beautiful but spaghetti could be improved.' There I will begin training so that I may join your Clowns Without Borders. It seems that war will not end soon and they are in need of some performing doctors. Tony and Lupe must stay here in Los Angeles through Manny's recovery, and certainly through the trial. Magdelena has secured an audition with Cirque du Soleil,

as they do not know her true age. Paula intends to catch a
Green Tortoise bus south to Mexico with a lady friend she has
encountered. Madre has at last saved the money she needs to
move to San Francisco and launch her comedy levitation drag
show. My proposition to you is that you should join me on my
journey, that it should in fact become our journey because we
are *famiglia*. As mythical husband and wife, you will be welcome in Italia. You will be welcome in all of Europe, in fact. As
mythical husband and wife, we will be welcome to return to
this country as well. If a man loves America—even if he loves it
with a broken heart as I do—it is important to have a green
card. This much I have learned. So, you see, with this ring, I
propose to you a world without borders."

I think of the single smiling face in the newspaper, the
Clowns Without Borders. I think of Umbria, the vast golden
landscapes where everything smelled of garlic and easy faith. I
could travel to Assisi again. This time in the dark and chilled
basement of the basilica, I would touch the tomb. I think of
the way I loved Barbaro before I knew him to be messed up
and scared, hollow and sorry. The love I feel for him now is
hurt and enduring, the kind of love that isn't afraid of the
harsh and dreadful gifts that surely await us. "But I'm not a
doctor and I'm not a clown." I look down at my hands, pink
scars already fading. "I don't have a talent anymore. That day
you came and ate with us at Dorothy's cabin on the lake—I
made that dinner myself. I worked for the wine and I caught
the fish and I collected the herbs and I fried the bread. I can't
bleed anymore, not even if I want to."

"As you wish," Barbaro says softly, moving to put the ring
back in his pocket.

I watch his flickering shadow on the wall behind him.

"However," he says, "I should tell you that I have been in contact with the Free University in Umbria, and there are many clowns to be fed. I will understand if the work of a cook is not worthy of you, but I desired to extend the invitation. For drama, Frankka, but for love, too."

Mythical husband and wife. Barbaro's words settle like blueberries on my tongue. A sudden and absurd shared context. An anchor in the grand confrontation between mystery and literalism in which mystery always wins out.

I hold out my hand, fingers outstretched, to receive his sparkling fiction. "I'd be delighted to be your mythical wife."

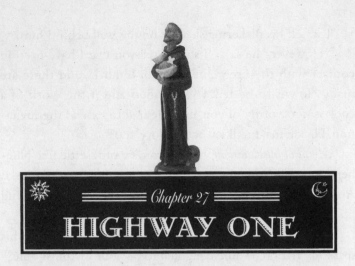

Chapter 27

HIGHWAY ONE

Francis of Assisi

(WHEN YOU'RE READY FOR YOUR NEW LIFE)

A.K.A. il Poverello

FEAST DAY: October 4

SYMBOLS: birds, a wolf, a deer

Before his conversion, Francis of Assisi had a reputation for being a liar, a thief, a drunk, a womanizer, a party animal, and a madman with a penchant for running naked through the streets.

Rich rebel boy, he burned through his dad's cash, showed no interest in the family silk trading business.

When he was twenty, war broke out between Assisi and neighboring Perugia. Francis eagerly took up arms and rode off, dreaming of glory. But the reality of war is nothing glorious. He survived the carnage and several months as a prisoner, then staggered home, sick and broken. He took to wandering the outskirts of town, was horrified by the squalor in which most people lived.

The greed of some, which causes the poverty of so many. The messes the people of this world get into. Unbelievable. The arguments and the battles and almost all of them because one side or the other can't understand the concept of a metaphor.

Out riding one day, Francis came upon a leper begging at the roadside. He dismounted. Careful to remain at arm's length, he gave the poor deformed man a few coins. Then, pushed by some invisible hand, he knelt down and kissed the leper.

From that kiss, his destiny began to take shape. He started visiting the sick, giving them whatever he had. His father accused him of stealing from the family's warehouse, had his son arrested and dragged before the bishop in the town square. But Francis wasn't one for tough love. He apologized for giving away what wasn't his, then stripped himself of his fancy clothes and threw them at his speechless father. He renounced his inheritance, saying, "Hitherto I have called you Father on earth, but now I say Our Father who art in heaven."

The bishop quickly covered Francis with an undyed brown peasant's frock, and the transformation from rich rebel boy to monk was complete.

Folks ridiculed Francis, but no one could deny his subversive appeal. He possessed nothing, wasn't handsome or tall—he stood about five-foot-four. He offered no great learning or wisdom, often went hungry, but men and women from all walks of life felt compelled to follow him, giving away their money and wandering poor with this radically joyful holy nutball.

The seekers lived outside or in makeshift shelters, worked in the fields in exchange for food, tended the sick, comforted the depressed.

Francis fed all the tame birds of his community, and they gathered to hear him preach. In one town, he subdued a wolf who was attacking people and livestock. He implored the villagers to feed their wolf so it wouldn't harm them anymore. They did, and that wolf wandered docile from door to door until the end of its days.

In his peasant's frock, Francis challenged the decadence of church government, preached a message of antimaterialism and compassionate service. He composed a rule based on the Gospel words about perfection, sought approval from Pope Innocent III. At first the pope thought the whole thing sounded outrageous, but then he had two dreams. In one, a palm tree grew at his feet. In the next, Francis propped up the Lateran church, which seemed about to collapse. "All right," Innocent finally said. "Preach your rule, but only by word of mouth."

In the summer of 1224, when Francis was forty-two years old, he retired in seclusion to a tiny hut, where he intended to suffer a long fast in honor of the archangel Michael. He requested that he be left alone for six weeks, but after just a month, on the feast of the Exaltation of the Holy Cross, as he contemplated the Passion so intensely he believed himself transformed into Christ, an angel appeared. Its fiery wings descended from heaven, and within their folds the crucified Savior appeared. Francis was frightened and ecstatic, uplifted and heartrended. Emerging from the vision, he was amazed to find his hands and feet marked with bent nails, his side wounded and bleeding.

For the remaining two years of his life, Francis kept his hands in his habit, his feet covered by shoes and stockings. He composed his "Canticle of the Sun," set it to music, and on his last living day, he asked his friends and followers to sing that part of the canticle that honors death. He broke bread with his community, was laid on the earth to preach to them a last time, and to bless them.

> *Praised be You, my Lord, through Sister Death,*
> *from whom no one living can escape.*
> *Woe to those who die in mortal sin!*
> *Blessed are they She finds doing Your Will.*
> *No second death can do them harm.*
> *Praise and bless my Lord and give Him thanks,*
> *And serve Him with great humility.*

Turn to Francis when it's time to detox and transform your pointless gorging antics into a glorious quest. Pray for the opportunity to do maximum good in the world. Honor the saint with your radical joy. Sing to Brother Sun, Sister Moon, and Mother Earth, who sustains and governs you. You'll never be an orphan again. Strip yourself of your arrogance and run through the streets naked and shouting: "I am filled with enthusiasm for my mystical adventure!"

Car tires on asphalt, skid marks on the median. The road ribbons up the wild coast, clinging to rugged cliffs where land meets sea. Eastern hills the color of wet jade rise over my right shoulder. Sheer overhangs made of clay, just waiting for landslides. A single slip of the wheel could send us careening over the edge into power-mad surf. I keep my eyes on the yellow lines even as the Pacific crashes breathtaking indigo foam white.

Is there anything in this world so heartbreakingly gorgeous as the drive up from Los Angeles and Santa Barbara, through Las Cruces and Guadalupe, past San Luis Obispo and San Simeon, toward Santa Cruz and San Francisco? No wonder this land has been stolen a thousand times. It was mine once—I took it. Then it was taken from me.

In a sandy lot that smells of eucalyptus, we pull over to feed the birds. We're seagulls and geese, lighthouses and salty air. It's just Barbaro, Pia, and me heading north in the painted caravan. We've left our fellow travelers in southern California, left Tony and Lupe with most of our money to help through Manny's recovery, left Paula and her lady friend waiting at a Green Tortoise stop for the bus that will take them south, far away from Baltimore, left Magdelena with her platinum dreams of stardom—she'll fly across grand circus stages like a bird in the firmament.

There's a good wind off the ocean as we pile back into the truck. I'm in the driver's seat, Pia next to me, Barbaro juggling oranges in back. Even with my foot aching tender and bandaged, I'm still the better driver. In San Francisco, we'll leave Pia and her truck at a punk house in the Mission District, where she knows someone who knows someone. We'll spend the night at the hostel pinch-faced Sister

Mehitable started after she finally retired from All Saints K–8. And in the morning, we'll crawl up Van Ness to the Civic Center, then take a Muni bus to the giant passport office, which probably won't look so giant to me now.

Pia smiles at me. She's wearing purple lipstick and a big white wedding dress she bought at St. Vincent de Paul in Los Angeles. "We've come a long way together," she says.

Seven years.

She slips a Loretta Lynn tape into the player.

"I bet you never miss Mesa."

"Sure," she says. "I miss every place I've ever been."

"Even Sacramento?"

She winks at me. "Even Sacramento."

I think of what Dorothy said: *We're all Christ and we all get crucified.* In school they taught me that Jesus died for my sins, but I guess it's a little bit more complicated than that.

"Listen," I say to Madre, "do you mind if we stop at the Holy Cross Cemetery in Santa Cruz?"

"'Course I don't mind, hon."

So we exit on Soquel Avenue, take a left on Seventh.

The sun is doing its setting thing, turning the city into a vast bouquet of roses.

Pia and Barbaro offer to come inside with me, but I shake my head no. "I won't be long," I promise.

The mausoleum complexes loom, dark gray crosses and colorful murals depicting the life of Christ set into concrete-gray walls. My parents' bones are in these crypts, filed away like old tax forms.

On the far side of the third square structure, I easily find their plaque, stand silent before their names. Ghosts the color of moonlit water and tangerine-scented regrets huddle behind me, and I can feel all my blood coursing through all my veins.

I say, "You know, guys, that was a dumb thing to do, crashing the car. But I know how it is sometimes. A single slip of the wheel. No warning signs beyond that creeping road weariness you ignore. They never told us how faintly prophecy could whisper. I always imagined the voice of God would come booming from some pulpit in the sky, but it's quiet as wind." I look down at my feet, one bandaged, one booted. "Nana turned out to be all right as guardians go, but I guess you knew that. I guess you knew everything would work out the way it was supposed to—or at least that it would work out somehow. I hope you didn't die in mortal sin or anything. I hear that's a drag. I could say a prayer for you now. I bet you have no idea how many prayers I can still recite by heart: Our Father, Mea Culpa, Hail Mary, Glory Be, O Lady of Perpetual Help, Most High, All Powerful, That You Would Bless Me Indeed, Holy this and Holy that. If only there were a special Catholic *Jeopardy,* I'd win big. You know I would. I'd make you proud. Anyway, listen. If you see Nana, tell her thanks for me, okay?"

I place both my hands on the wall of the tomb, close my eyes.

My parents lie silent in their crypt. Maybe they're singing with angels in some High Sierra hideaway, but I can't hear them.

It's true that I never processed that loss, but maybe I never wanted to. There's a hollowness in me, a vacant stone cave where only dreams sleep, but I'm getting used to it. Deliciously empty. I look down at my palms, my healing scars. I hope they never disappear entirely.

I limp back out to the car, climb into the driver's seat. Barbaro pokes his head into the cab. "I almost forgot," he says. "I have for you a new saint book." A smile flickers the corners of his lips as he holds out a gold-covered journal. "You will tell me a story?"

Plus:

Plus: Insights, Interviews, and More

Don't Try This at Home:
An Incomplete History of
the Stigmata

*He that believeth in me, the works that I do,
shall he do; and greater than these he shall do.*

—John: 14:12

Believe nothing. Entertain possibilities.

—Caroline W. Casey

If you get the Stigmata, the Ph.D. of Catholic mysticism, you're already halfway to sainthood—just so long as they don't haul you off to the county mental hospital first.

The stigmata, wounds corresponding to those suffered by Jesus during the Passion and Crucifixion appear spontaneously on the body of a believer and can disappear in the space of a few hours or linger for decades. There are plenty of differences among stigmatics when it comes to the number and placement of their wounds—some have had all five marks, some only a shoulder wound representing the one Jesus suffered while carrying the cross, and some have lesions matching the crown of thorns. Some stigmatics bleed from their palms and feet, corresponding to the common artistic depictions of the crucifixion; others bleed from their wrists and ankles, matching the points on the body where historians believe Jesus was nailed to the cross.

There are actually two kinds of stigmata in Catholic tradition: visible and invisible. While praying before a crucifix in 1375, Catherine of Siena saw five rays of blood emanating from Christ's wounds and coming toward her. She knew what was happening and asked God to make her stigmata invisible to the world. As the rays reached her body, they changed into shafts of light. She suffered the pain, then, without the bloody mess or the freak-show attention.

But let's focus on the stigmata even atheists can see.

Now, stigmata blood doesn't smell salty and metallic the way normal blood does, and the lacerations don't get that fetid scent like your average festering wounds. No, this blood smells like jasmine. Or roses. And in some cases, the blood type of the stigmata has been found not to match that of the sufferer. It is understood as being truly the blood of Christ. But rosy scent or none, the stigmata isn't for wimps. The wounds are often heralded by depression, weakness, and a great deal of pain. Some stigmatics even report feeling whips across their back. *Ouch.*

Because the wounds correspond with the death of Christ, they often appear during the holy days before Easter, and then disappear on Easter itself.

The first widely documented case of the stigmata was Saint Francis of Assisi's back in 1224. Already old and sick, Francis had an ecstatic vision of a six-winged angel embracing a crucified man. Afterward, and until his death two years later, Francis bore the marks on his hands, feet, and side. Early accounts described dark scars that bled periodically.

Since Saint Francis, there have been some five hundred reported cases of the stigmata. Their existence is well-enough documented that it's no longer a subject of hot debate. Still, hard-core skeptics figure the injuries are always self-inflicted. And there *have* been cases of attention-seeking holy self-mutilators over the years. Poor Magdalena de la Cruz, a sixteenth-century Franciscan nun in Spain, was honored as a living saint before she confessed that it was all a hoax. I guess life can get boring in the convent—you can hardly blame a cloistered nun for pulling a wacky publicity stunt every now and again— but even stigmatics who've been examined extensively by doctors have had a hard time getting anyone to take them seriously.

When Berthe Mrazek, a Brussels-born lion tamer and circus performer, added the stigmata to her repertoire in the early 1900s, she ended up in an insane asylum. More recently, in the mid-1980s, Gigliola Giorgini was convicted of fraud by an Italian court. Were Berthe and Gigliola quacks? Probably. But virtually every stigmatic in history has been challenged as either a lunatic or a fraud.

A common theme in the biographies of these mystics, after all, is that even before the wounds appeared, they were all a little bit loony. There's a fine line between mysticism and madness. Even Saint Francis and Padre Pio—both widely believed to have received the wounds of Christ as a result of true mystical experiences—were also well-known nut cases in their youths.

And consider the modern-day Father James Bruse, an unassuming associate pastor at St. Elizabeth Ann Seton Church in Virginia. His pre-ordination life included a stunt that got him into the 1978 *Guinness Book of World Records:* he rode a roller coaster for five days straight! He became a Roman Catholic priest the following year and, in the early 1990s, he not only experienced the stigmata, but discovered religious statues weeping in his presence.

Some people get all the excitement.

Other commonalities in the lives of stigmatics include a penchant for fasting (pronounced "eating disorder" in modern psychiatric language) and self-flagellation (or self-mutilation). Teresa Neumann, for example, a German mystic and stigmatic, survived solely on communion wafers from 1926 to 1962. And Saint Catherine of Siena began refusing food at the age of seven, often went without sleep, and reportedly beat herself daily. Had she come of age in twenty-first-century America, her antics might well have earned her a bed in the psych ward and a prescription for Paxil.

Psychologists point out that eating disorders and self-mutilation—like the stigmata itself—are significantly more common in women than in men. Some researches have even associated the wounds with Munchausen syndrome. But self-inflicted stigmata heal naturally. In the more widely accepted cases

Plus: **Insights, Interviews, and More**

of mystical stigmata, blood flows freely and cannot be cured or stopped with traditional medical intervention.

One curious theory put forth by skeptics who nonetheless agree that not all stigmatics are sitting in their cells driving nails into their hands and feet is that the wounds are *psychically* self-inflicted. It's sort of a new age "power of positive thinking," "believe and achieve" argument. It's a place where paradox-embracing mystics and logic-dependent scientists can come to agree about something they can't quite explain. They call it the "theological placebo effect." This theory holds that a powerful imagination engaged in intense prayer can manifest just about anything. It neither affirms nor denies the existence of a divine intelligence, so it's a handy compromise at otherwise-awkward family dinners.

Virtually all stigmatics are Roman Catholics, and a majority have been cloistered nuns or priests. These little factoids please skeptics to no end. Surely Christ would pick the occasional Jew or Protestant to pierce, would he not? But music students are rarely given Ph.Ds in mathematics. These wounds are part of the Catholic mystical tradition and experience.

Within that tradition, stigmata has been reported in dozens of countries, and the recipients have ranged from Dominican priests to Poor Clare nuns and from Cuban teenagers to Midwestern grandfathers. There are famous saints such as Francis of Assisi, Catherine of Genoa, John of God, Rita of Cascia, Marie of the Incarnation, and Padre

Pio. But laypeople get the stigmata, too. Irma Izquierdo was nineteen years old when she received the wounds. She'd been known at her school in the Consolacíon region of Cuba for being rather pious, but her classmates didn't know that Irma saw strange winged beings in the school corridors. Shortly before Easter in 1956, she lost her appetite and started having vivid dreams filled with Catholic symbolism. She tried to ignore the visions, but she couldn't ignore this: she suddenly "saw" the passions and the crucifixion in her mind's eye with such clarity she felt herself to be fully present at the event. She experienced being nailed to the cross and pierced at her side as though it were all happening to her. Shaken, she sought medical help, but doctors told her she was hallucinating. In the days before Easter, the five classic wounds appeared on her hands, feet, and side.

One of the most famous current stigmatics is the moon-faced Giorgio Bongiovanni, a Catholic member of an Italian UFO cult who received the wounds on his hands and forehead during a visit to Fatima in 1989. His religious lesions can't be explained by doctors and, according to several news reports, they appear and disappear at will.

Emiliano Aden, a young Argentinian stigmatic has described the prelude to his first episode, saying, "It felt like something was moving on my skin." He then felt a burning sensation like heat from a fire. "I saw a tap in a garden and went to wet my head," he recalled. "When the water touched me, I felt as if my head was opening." At first, the lacerations on his wrists simply bled, but soon crosses appeared and the blood felt cold. Emiliano's stigmata now appears intermittently. He describes the pain as "more like an inner pain, not borne from the wrists but from my heart."

Another Argentinian stigmatic, Gladys Quiroga de Motta, was just a shy housewife before she started getting messages from Our Lady and received the wounds of Christ in the early 1980s. These days, Gladys entertains pilgrims and shares her messages from the Blessed Virgin Mary.

And on Ash Wednesday in 1993, Francis, a midwestern great-grandfather who uses only his first name, was asked by Jesus if he would accept suffering.

Be careful what you agree to.

Forty days later, swelling on the top and bottom of his hands broke open and bled profusely.

He ain't the Messiah, but folks wait in line for hours to see him, and his healing powers are well-known to his devotees. In 1995, Kathy Crombie, a "marginal" Catholic who had "issues" with the church, took her teenaged son to see Francis on the suggestion of a friend. Chad Crombie had found a lump in his neck shortly after graduating from high school and been diagnosed with Hodgkin's lymphoma.

Nothing to lose, Chad agreed to go and see the holy man in Flint, Michigan.

Kathy later described Francis's wounds to a reporter as "huge—about the size of a silver dollar—deep, deep purple-red, scabbed-over wounds. On the back of his hands were Band-Aids and you could see blood under them."

When Francis put his hand on Chad, he felt "a chill more electric than cold" that shot straight through him. He felt completely relaxed.

When mother and son got back in their car, they were overwhelmed by the smell of roses. Chad's hand automatically went to his neck. And miraculously, the lump was gone.

Years later, there's still no sign of the Hodgkin's disease.

Now there's something that'll make you start praying your rosary again.

But before you start praying to manifest the wounds of Christ yourself, be forewarned: simply exhibiting the stigmata won't get you canonized. If you want to be honored in the Vatican's hall of fame, you'll have to start performing some real miracles. Heal the sick. Feed the poor and ask the powers that be why they have no food. Develop a love strategy. And embrace the radical notion that you can please God by being simply and untheatrically yourself.

A Reader's Group Guide

1. When we are first introduced to Frankka in the prologue, she immediately categorizes herself as a lapsed, or recovering, Catholic. Did this categorization make you more drawn toward Frankka as a character or did you respond negatively to that phrase? What does it mean to be a recovering Catholic? How do you relate to her?

2. A recurring emotional conflict in *The Traveling Death and Resurrection Show* is the tension Frankka feels between her "wondering faith" and the stricter belief system she grew up with. Do you think Frankka successfully reconciles this conflict in the course of the book? Do any of her other travelers seem to struggle with this same issue? How do they resolve it? Do you still hold the same beliefs you were taught by your parents? Why or why not?

3. After being orphaned at a young age, Frankka begins to search to find a place where she truly belongs. After she's been traveling with the show for over seven years, it becomes clear that her fellow misfits have become a sort of surrogate family for her. Have you ever experienced this kind of community? What would be your second family?

4. If you are a person of faith, where do you fall on the spectrum between religious literalism and mysticism?

5. Which of Frankka's saint stories did you relate to the most? Have you ever gotten creative with an element of your religion? Can you share how you did it and what your motivation was? How does such creativity help or hinder faith?

6. "You can't just take the parts of a religion you like," Tony tells Madre Pia in Chapter five. What parts of Catholicism did Frankka embrace? Which parts did she run from? Do you agree with Tony? Why?

7. What do you think is the significance of the tunnel leading from the church to the old minister's house?

8. When Frankka is in the mountains, she muses that Dorothy might represent a waking dream—her intrinsic loneliness manifesting a caretaker. Considering that Frankka's experience includes visitations from saints, do you interpret Dorothy to be a normal human being or could she be some kind of visitation? Does it make a difference to the story?

9. What does Dorothy mean when she tells Frankka, "We're all Christ and we all get crucified"?

10. Frankka seems to protect herself with a certain inaccessibility. Does this

remoteness make her harder to like? Why might she make herself hard to know?

11. Why do you think Frankka loses her "talent"?

12. In light of the basic theories regarding the stigmata—that they are either self-inflicted, relate to a mental disorder. manifest themselves psychosomatically by a powerful imagination engaged in prayer, or are the result of direct contact with the Divine—how would you classify Frankka's stigmata?

13. If you could have one mystical talent, what would it be?

13 Questions with Ariel Gore

1. *Who would play Frankka in the ideal movie version of* **The Traveling Death and Resurrection Show?** *What about Madre Pia? Barbaro?*

   Frankka: Can Lili Taylor look 28? If not, Christina Ricci
   Madre Pia: Rikki Lake
   Barbaro: Adrien Brody or Gael Garcia Bernal could both do it, though really differently. Maybe Adrien would be better.

2. *Name the four people—living or dead— you would like most to invite to a dinner party at your house. What would you cook?*

   Haruki Murakami, Gertrude and Alice, Jorge Luis Borges. Order out and pretend that I made it.

3. *Are you a cat person or a dog person?*

   I've had it with all my pets.

4. *Of the seven deadly sins (pride, envy, gluttony, lust, anger, greed, and sloth), which one is the hardest for you to resist?*

   Gluttony.

Little Red Riding Hood

by Ariel Gore, 1974

*The ocean shone
   white and blue
While Little Red
   Riding Hood was
   watching it.
The sun was almost to
   land on the ground.
Run, run, run, run.
Then she went home
   and her mother
   said,
"Take these cookies to
   your grandma."
Then she met a wolf.
But it wasn't a wolf,
   it was her Daddy.*

5. *What are you reading right now?*

Autobiography of a Blue-Eyed Devil by Inga Muscio and *Lizard* by Banana Yoshimoto

6. *What is your favorite book of all time?*

I think I'm going to go with *The Wind-Up Bird Chronicle.*

7. *Coffee or tea?*

Coffee

8. *What was the vision, inspiration, or event that first caused you to start writing this story?*

Two traveling adventures: a west-coast book tour with a band and a shadow puppet show, then a summer in Italy wandering saint sites.

9. *What do you consider your first real piece of writing?*

Little Red Riding Hood.

10. *What is your favorite memory?*

Underwater childhood. Either Silver Lake or the Pacific Ocean.

11. *If you could live in another time and place, when and where would that be?*

Shanghai, first half of the twentieth century. Kill me off before the Cultural Revolution.

12. *Who is your oldest friend?*

Julia from junior high school. We used to go jogging together and then get drunk before first period.

13. *What do **you** consider the absolute most important question to ask someone when you want to find out their deepest and most heartfelt identity?*

What were you before you were a gender?

Plus: Insights, Interviews, and More

About the Author

The daughter of an excommunicated Roman Catholic priest, Ariel Gore grew up attending her dad's rebel Catholic church in the San Francisco Bay Area. She left home at age sixteen and spent the years she was supposed to be in high school as an international bag lady traveling through Asia and Europe. She gave birth to her daughter—not immaculately conceived—in rural Italy and returned to California at age nineteen, baby in tow.

Following her misspent youth, she became addicted to caffeine and earned degrees from Mills College and the University of California at Berkeley, started the award-winning parenting zine *Hip Mama*, authored three parenting books, then up and moved north. Her lyrical vagabond memoir, *Atlas of the Human Heart*, was a finalist for the Oregon Book Award in 2004. A veteran of several west-coast road shows, she drafted *The Traveling Death and Resurrection Show* in three miraculously child-free kamikaze writing weeks in a farmhouse in Italy. When not manically traversing the globe, she teaches creative writing in Portland, Oregon.

She thanks you for contributing to her daughter's college fund by purchasing this book and sincerely hopes you enjoyed the show.